Also by Rechan

Handcuffs & Lace
Will of the Alpha (editor)
Taboo (editor)
Will of the Alpha 2 (editor)
Will of the Alpha 3 (editor)
Dungeon Grind (co-editor)
Intimate Little Secrets

FERAL!

Edited by Rechan

Feral!

Production © Rechan and FurPlanet Productions

"Snowbound" © 2018 Of The Wilds
"Supernatural Delight" © 2018 Whyte Yoté
"Nothing Feathered, Nothing Gained" © 2018 Resolute
"Adrenaline High" © 2018 Kandrel

Cover illustration by Rukis

Published by FurPlanet Productions
Dallas, TX
http://www.FurPlanet.com

Print ISBN 978-1-61450-413-9
Electronic ISBN 978-1-61450-414-6

Printed in the United States of America
First Edition Trade Paperback 2018

TABLE OF CONTENTS

Snowbound   7
    Of The Wilds

Supernatural Delight   57
    Whyte Yoté

Nothing Feathered, Nothing Gained   83
    Resolute

Adrenaline High   117
    Kandrel

About the Authors   133

Snowbound

Of The Wilds

"What month is it?"

Blinding snow swirled around Rhin in ceaseless white cascades. It crusted her tattered, feather-lined cloak, and crunched beneath her worn-out boots. Even through three layers of wool socks, Rhin's feet were still cold. The wind numbed her nose, smothering all scent. Tiny icicles edged her vision, where warm breath brushed the fringes of her hood. Rhin shifted her heavy pack, and her cook pot clanked against her canteen. Her shoulders ached, but at least she rarely got travel blisters anymore.

"Not sure. Bright Sun, maybe? I've never done well with time."

It should have been summer, Rhin knew that much. But years of surviving an empty world after the seasons died blurred the days together. A week was easy to count, but a month was harder, and a year was nearly impossible. Lately, she marked time by notching the sheepskin map she found on a dead legionnaire in a ruined shack.

At the crest of a windswept hill, Rhin took temporary shelter behind a copse of dead trees. Beads of ice clung to skeletal boughs clattering in the wind. Rhin unslung her pack, and dug out a scroll case bound in leather. She opened it, and unfurled the map kept inside, bracing it against a tree. Rhin added up the notches and scowled. If her count was right, she had followed that chart into the mountains for months now.

Rhin tucked the map away, grimacing. At least she was almost there. The map led to an Outer Legion fort hidden deep in the mountains. All that was left now were a few more rugged, wooded foothills. As Rhin trudged on, she was heartened to see a few glimpses of green needles beneath the white shroud enveloping the trees. Portions of the pine forest here still clung to life. A spark of hope ignited in Rhin's heart, and she hugged herself beneath her cloak. Maybe there were human survivors here, too.

How long had it been since she'd heard a voice that wasn't her own?

Soon, she caught her first glimpse of the fort. The boxy stone structure stood in the distance, a looming gray ghost scarcely visible through the snow. Just the sight of it left her heart racing. With renewed energy, she hurried towards the stone wall encircling the outpost.

No guards manned the walls, and a crumpled watchtower blocked the entryway. She used the debris to help scale the wall, her pack's contents rattling. Rhin clambered down into the courtyard, and gazed around. The squarish fort was built right into the mountainside's granite heart. Carts and wagons lay buried in the snow between crumbling outbuildings. Big drifts covered the fortress's main gates. Windows were blocked off from within, and no light shone from them. She saw no sign of the colorful ribbons used to mark gravesites in the early days after the first freeze.

The ember of warm hope in Rhin's heart faded back into cold ash. This place looked as empty as all the rest. Rhin took a deep breath and let it out in a long, slow sigh. The last time her desperate hope for survivors had led only to desolation, she cried all night. This time the emptiness just numbed her, as if the unending chill had finally reached her very soul.

"At least you still have me to talk to."

"Shut up, Echo. I'm not in the mood."

"Sorry. Look at it this way. No survivors might mean more supplies."

Her echo was right.

With the help of her map, Rhin found a small, concealed stairway carved into the stone. She ascended the icy steps carefully, brushing away the snow. At the top, she discovered a thick wooden door tucked away in an alcove. The door's faded and flecked pale blue paint was the only splash of color in the white world. Rhin tested the handle, but it was either locked, frozen, or both. She took a deep breath, and threw her shoulder against the wood. The door budged, and after a few more attempts, it popped open.

Rhin stumbled into darkness. After she caught her balance, she gazed around. Snow blew inside and danced in the beams of ghostly light seeping in through cracks in boarded up windows. After so much time outdoors, the air inside felt unnaturally still, barely warmer and tainted by a stagnant mustiness. Rhin turned to examine the door. Heavy bolts lined it and she doubted they were there to keep out thieves. The Outer Legion guarded borders against man and beast alike. Not much frightened them.

"Why weren't they set?" Rhin closed the door then worked her sword free. "Maybe they went for firewood, got caught in a flash freeze."

Her heart pounded as she unslung her pack. She crouched down, listening. The silence felt eerie, an echoing uncertainty lingering in abandoned halls. Rhin dug her lantern out of her pack, then drew her long knife, and struck it with a piece of flint. The *clack* made her wince, but she repeated the action till spark took hold in her lamp. The wavering, orange glow revealed the undecorated stone walls of an antechamber, and a long corridor with several wooden doors flaking their paint away.

"Sure, tell the monsters where you are, Rhin."

"There's no monsters here." She kept her voice soft.

"Then why are you whispering?"

"Just in case."

Rhin crept down the hall, her lamplight an orange spirit dancing on every surface. The melted remnants of candles adorned tarnished brass sconces, with red wax rivulets frozen halfway down the walls.

When Rhin reached the first door, she found it ajar, and pushed it open with her sword. The creaking protest of rusted hinges left her cringing. She half-expected some shapeless monstrosity to lunge out, but the room proved empty. A bed with a simple, straw-filled mattress sat along one wall, and some of the straw poked out where small creatures had dug through it.

"Rats, maybe. Or squirrels. They'd be tastier."

The corridor led past more quarters filled only with moldering furniture and remnants of forgotten lives. Eventually, the hall spilled into a cavernous chamber. Arched wooden beams spanned the towering ceiling, bronze lamps adorned walls, and scuffs on the floor marked where Rhin suspected a grand table once stood. Old tomes lay scattered beneath shelves on either side of a massive granite-brick hearth blackened by decades of soot.

Her heart leapt when she saw the fireplace. "Oh, Gods, I can build *such* a fire there." She checked the lamps, then set flame to one that still held oil. Rhin crouched to examine the scratches on the floor. "Musta dragged their table to the hearth to burn it. Woulda lasted longer than the books, but why not go out for firewood?"

She scowled as she rose and made her way to the fort's front gates. The entryway was built large enough for supply wagons to be brought inside for the long winters. Now, three sturdy cross-beams barred the gates. Rhin brushed her fingers over one of the reinforcements. They looked newer than the gates themselves. The Legion often fought dragons, but stories passed among the early survivors spoke of things far worse, unleashed by whatever forces had sundered the seasons. Rhin had never seen them herself, but this was not the first time she discovered fortifications seemingly added *after* the freeze.

Rhin struggled to avoid thinking about what they were keeping out as she continued her search. A winding stairwell led to the upper floor where intersecting hallways connected to more barracks and individual quarters. At the far end of the hall, a door painted dark red drew her attention. The golden sigil of the Outer Legion was embossed upon the door, along with the name and rank of the fort's commander.

"This looks promising."

The door was unlocked, and she opened it cautiously, sword at the ready. Rhin sucked in a breath when she saw the commander yet lingered in his bed, long dead. One arm lay draped across the diamond-patterned, purple and gold blankets pulled up over his chest. A hint of rot tinted the air, but the cold left his corpse frozen, and half mummified.

"Poor old bastard." Rhin sheathed her sword and set her lantern aside. She settled on the bed. "Bet you sent your men to another outpost, hoping to save them. Stayed behind to fulfill your Legion oath. Brave, old man, but honor, courage, or cowardice, they all get us killed."

Rhin patted the dead man's frozen leg under the blanket. "Commander Jevva, right? Pleasure to meet you. I'm Rhin." She glanced at Jevva's face. "Don't suppose you knew a Captain Ger? I served with him. No, I'm not in the Legion. Never took the oath. Sellsword, myself." She held up her hand. "I know, I know. Bad reputation. But I helped Ger and his men slay a few dragons, avenge a few villages. He was a good man. First freeze got him." Rhin's hand trembled, and she dropped it into her lap before hunching over. Her voice shook. "Think I'm the only one left, now."

She took a deep breath to settle her nerves, only for rot's sickly-sweet odor to make her gag. Fighting back nausea, Rhin gazed around. Ashes lingered amidst the soot-caked bricks of a small fireplace. Maps and books smothered a semi-circular desk. More animal hides and fur blankets than Rhin had ever seen covered the walls and floor. Several heavy cloaks lined with the silver-white pelts of arctic foxes hung from hooks.

"Gonna have to help myself to those cloaks." Rhin rubbed the blanket. It was soft, filled with down. "And this. Better see what else you got."

Rhin rose and went to the dead commander's desk. She dug

through books and documents, tossing whatever she didn't need on the floor. When she discovered the commander's supply log, she delicately turned through the brittle pages. The most recent entries described moving foodstuffs into an underground storage room, warmed by a hot spring. They had crates of biscuits and hardtack, dried and salted meats and fish, sacks of grain, and even some medicines. Better still, they had wine.

"Wine?" Rhin laughed and jumped in place. "You have *wine!*"

Continuing her search, Rhin found a regional survey map showing the myriad other springs that riddled the area. Deep in the valley beneath the mountains, enough hot water bubbled up to shroud the lowlands in clouds of warm steam. According to the notes, it once kept the temperatures above freezing even in the heart of winter.

Rhin slumped onto the commander's bed, her mind spinning. If that was still true, there could be vegetation, animals, maybe even survivors. *Or monsters.* Rhin rubbed her hands over her face. It didn't matter. The lingering hope of hearing another voice was the only fragile thread left tying her to sanity. If there was even the smallest chance...

"You gotta know, Rhin."

Once more, her echo was right. She *had* to know.

"Tonight, you sleep in comfort." She eased back to her feet, and tugged the blanket away from the dead man. "Build a big fire, eat biscuits and fish, sleep in a real bed, and drink till you pass out. And when the weather eases? You're going to that valley."

***

Wrapped in warm clothes looted from the fort, Rhin pushed through curtains of heavy snow. It had taken her three days of travel just to reach the valley's edge. The commander's maps and reports proved invaluable in finding shelter on her journey. They also provided warning. No one he sent to investigate whether the valley was still warm had returned.

"Dragons probably got them." She passed her sword back and forth between her gloved hands, spinning the blade to keep her fingers warm. "That's what they fought out here, before all this."

"Remember when *dragons* were the only scourge?" Rhin danced a few steps through the powdery snow. "At least dragons could talk, when they weren't trying to kill us."

She jabbed finger in the air. "*Me.* Not us. Just...keep that straight."

"You're losing it, Rhin."

"No shit, Echo."

When the hills were nearly behind her, Rhin paused to check her map. By the end of the day, she should be nearing the edges of the valley's lowlands. With any luck, she thought, she might even stumble upon some greenery soon. As much as she wanted fresh meat, she would be even happier to fill up her pack with any sort of edible vegetation or medicinal plants.

As she tucked her map way, Rhin thanked her mother for being such a knowledgeable woman. Her mother was a wanderer who settled in a village with Rhin's father. As Rhin grew up, her mother taught her how to live off the land and use a sword and bow. That extensive knowledge helped her survive long after blind luck saved her from the first freeze.

Beyond the hills, Rhin passed through a dead forest, shrouded in thick fog. Barren trees loomed through the icy haze, countless monuments to a once-thriving woodland. Their trunks had a strange, shimmering appearance. Rhin soon realized it was ice, left by the mist. Skeletal limbs torn away by the ice's weight protruded from the snow like brown claws tearing through their white funeral veil.

A silhouette in the fog drew her attention, and she squinted as she tried to make it out. It was unnaturally boxy, with a strange, rounded shape at the top. Dread prickled at the base of her skull and trickled down her spine. Rhin eased her pack down and crept forward, gripping her sword tight. She cursed when she realized it was an upturned travel wagon. *Half* an upturned wagon. Rhin approached it and brushed snow off the side. The wood was painted the same blue as the fort's door. She scowled, and swept away more snow until part of the Outer Legion's symbol was visible.

"Guess we found the outpost's men."

"There you go with that 'we' shit again."

Rhin gazed around. The rest of the wagon was scattered in several pieces nearby. Further away, a second carriage lay on its side, partly buried under a snowdrift. Rhin clambered up the broken coach to peer inside. She didn't see anything useful, just snow and rust-hued stains on the wood. She hopped back down, wondering what attacked them. Clearing away more snow revealed gouges and shattered lumber. Rhin traced her fingers over a few of the gashes. Deep claw marks, but they didn't all look the same. Maybe there'd been an initial attack, and then—

Something moved in the fog. Snow crunched.

Her blood went cold. She turned her head a fraction of an inch. Past the wagon, something far larger than Rhin crept closer. *Shit!* She stepped around behind the carriage, hoping it hadn't noticed her. For a moment, there was silence again.

Then heavy footfalls thundered against the snow as the monster charged.

Rhin leapt away as the ruined wagon upended and crashed across the ground, missing her by a hair's breadth. Broken wood exploded and flew past her in splintered shards. Snow erupted everywhere. In an instant, the monster was upon her. Black claws swept through the air. Rhin darted just out of reach, acting on instinct.

A dragon. A sharp inhalation.

Fire was coming.

She dove and rolled under the dragon's head just as the beast sprayed flame across the frozen ground. The roar of dragon-fire met the hiss of snowmelt turning to steam. Beneath the beast, Rhin thrust her sword for his heart. The way the monster pivoted sent her blade deflecting off the segmented plates protecting his chest. Even before she could ready another blow, the dragon spun back towards her. Claws whistled through the air, aimed for her face. Rhin threw herself against the earth and the dragon stomped for her head.

Just in time, Rhin rolled away and lashed her sword at his foreleg. Steel caught against sturdy scales, forcing the dragon to pull his limb back. Rhin staggered to her feet, only for the dragon to twist away and swing his heavy tail at her. Once more, Rhin could only throw herself out of the way. The dragon's tail spines punched through a wagon wall, blasting shattered wood in all directions. In an instant, Rhin was on her feet and charging him from behind. She'd helped slay dragons, and remembered the Outer Legion's tactics.

Get under the belly, or get onto his back, and—

Inches before she got there, the dragon blasted fire again. This time he flattened his wings, and sprayed the liquid flame just above his back at her. Pain washed over Rhin, and it was all she could do to escape with only a scorched cloak and singed hair. She rolled across the snow, flames licking her. Rhin yanked at the ties to release her burning cloak. Somehow, she kept a grip on her sword.

For a second, she thought the world's unraveling must have driven the creature mad. Dragon scales were resilient but not impervious to fire, and their wings even less so. No dragon would risk burning themselves unless... In a moment of sickening fear, she realized the beast was baiting her. He wasn't crazy, he was experienced. He'd fought humans enough to learn their tactics.

No sooner was Rhin on her feet than the dragon was upon her. This time, she wasn't fast enough. The dragon's forepaw struck her so hard it lifted her off her feet. Sharp claws sliced through coat, clothes, and flesh alike, gouging her to her ribs. Rhin hit the ground and her vision flashed red. She tumbled across the snow. White-hot agony stole her breath.

Rhin fought the pain and rolled to all fours. She crawled across the snow to her sword. Blood soaked her clothes. As the dragon approached, she staggered to her knees. He was either out of fire, or didn't want to ruin his meal. She glared at him, her arms limp, fingers brushed her sword hilt in the snow, but she hesitated. Even as he drew back his foreleg, Rhin waited.

Only when his claws streaked for her head did Rhin act. At the last moment, she snatched up her sword and thrust it straight into the softest part of the dragon's paw. The blade pierced all the way through the bone and out the other side. Momentum wrenched the weapon from her grasp and tossed her back to the snow.

Agony bubbled in the dragon's scream as he stumbled away from her. Rhin's sword bobbled in his paw, wedged in the bone, and dark red blood gushed down his foreleg. With another anguished shriek, he collapsed. The beast reached for the sword with his other paw, limb shaking.

Hot pain rolled through Rhin as she drew the long knife from under her coat. She grit her teeth, focusing on survival. All she needed was an opening. The dragon tried to grasp the sword in his other paw, but only jarred the blade against the bone. He screeched, beating his tail on the snow.

When the monster lifted his bloodied, shaking foreleg to his muzzle, Rhin tensed, ready to pounce. The dragon took a few deep breaths, then bit the sword hilt. With teeth locked against it, he dragged his paw back down the blade. His clamped jaws muffled his tortured roar. Blood smeared over steel inch by inch, until the dragon's paw finally slid free. He spat the sword into the snow, and clutched his ruined paw to his chest plates, writhing.

Rhin seized her moment. Pushing through the pain, she closed the distance in an instant. Rhin flung herself onto the dragon's neck, just below the end of the spiny frill that ran down the back of his skull. She circled her arms around him, and pressed her dagger for his throat, the point catching where neck met lower jaw. Dragons were softer there, and she could open him deep enough to end him.

With her blade pressed against the dragon's throat, Rhin hesitated.

"Speak!" Rhin rasped her words, her blade trembling. "Athellian, can…can you speak the language?" Her throat tightened, and tears brimmed in her eyes. "Say something!"

"I'm not…" The dragon's words came in staggering pants, terrified but proud, "going to beg! I *won't* beg. So just do it, murderess!"

Rhin squeezed the handle of her dagger tightly. Waves of emotion and exhaustion swept over her and tears blurred her vision. After a few moments, wrecked by the first voice she'd heard in years, she dropped her knife. Her arms went slack, and overwhelmed by sudden sobs, she slipped off the dragon's neck into the snow. Pain faded, and her fear ebbed. In its place came a strange sort of relief.

She wasn't alone.

She wasn't the last.

The dragon shifted, his breathing pained and labored. Snow crunched. Rhin closed her eyes and waited, unafraid. Death couldn't be any colder than this. Only when she heard the dragon's footsteps getting softer did she open her eyes again. The dragon limped away, clutching his maimed paw to his chest. A trail of fresh blood marred the snow behind him.

He was leaving.

"Couldn't do it either, could he…" Rhin grimaced and sat up. She didn't want to talk to her echo anymore. She wanted to talk to someone real. "Please don't leave!"

The dragon stopped.

"My…my name is Rhin!"

Slowly, the dragon turned around.

"Do you have a name?"

"Elgaros." He stared at her across the bloody snow. "My name is Elgaros."

A name. A genuine name.

All at once, the dragon's details crystallized in her mind, as if his name made him real. His scales were green, a sickly, pale shade. He was too slender for a dragon, ribs pressed against his hide. Ridged black horns spiraled from his skull. Bronze-tipped spines lined the frills behind his pointed ears, and between his horns. More bronze marked his wings in uneven blotches. A cold, haunted look shone in his golden eyes.

He knew all the same horrors she did.

"Don't leave…"

Elgaros limped a single step towards her. "I fear we have killed each other."

Rhin knew he was right. He was losing blood, and facing likely infection. Hunting would be difficult, at best. And Rhin doubted she could make it home as wounded as she was. She crawled across the snow to rest against a section of broken wagon.

"It's nice to meet you anyway, Elgaros." She leaned her head back, smiling.

Elgaros lifted his paw, gazing at the jagged hole in it. A fresh trickle of blood coated his pale green scales. "I cannot say the same, Rhin."

Laughter bubbled from her, a joyous escape. "At least we don't have to die alone, now."

The dragon hobbled closer. He stared at her, then gave a long, drained sigh. "Perhaps that is best. I think I am ready for death. I am tired, and so weary of the cold."

"So am I. For what it's worth, I'm sorry."

"Matters not." Elgaros whimpered, then sucked in a breath, his whole muzzle contorted in pain.

"Would you talk to me? While we wait?" Rhin tilted her head back, staring at the falling snow. "I've hoped for years to just hear a voice again."

"Very well." The dragon eased onto his haunches, frills flattened. "It would be nice, to speak more before I die. I have not used words in some time."

"I talked to myself." Rhin cringed, glancing at her side. Blood drenched her coat. "Where've you been living? In the valley?"

"I did, until it grew too dangerous. Whatever monstrosities were unleashed when the world broke were drawn to what little warmth lingered there."

"So, they're real?" Rhin shifted, gritting her teeth against the pain.

"They are, and they hunt in the valley's fog. I live in a ruin, now. A *cold* ruin. I thought it safer." The dragon glanced at Rhin, rumbling what she could only describe as a bitter laugh. "But it seems it is dangerous here, too. A shame." He lay down in the snow, closing his eyes. "I had hoped to die somewhere warm."

Somewhere warm.

Rhin sat up straight. "I have a place. There's food and medicine left. I can't make it back on my own now, but maybe you could—"

"We are not friends!" The dragon cut her off with a snarl. "Your people killed us! I have done the same to men, and—"

"Doesn't matter." Rhin let out a long sigh, leaning her head back. "Everyone's gone. It's just us, now." She closed her eyes, her thoughts starting to drift. "Just us."

"So it is." Elgaros's voice softened. "What are you…offering?"

"A chance to die somewhere warm." Rhin forced herself to focus, opening her eyes. "And I could bind your paw, if you help me get there."

The dragon turned his head, gazing across the snow and fog. "I should like to feel warm again, before the end."

"Can you fly?"

"Yes, so long as I stay quite low. The higher clouds are icy and dangerous to my wings, now."

Gripping the carriage, Rhin dragged herself to her feet. "Then let me guide you. Please."

"So be it, human."

***

Rhin stirred the cookpot, one hand on her sword. She kept it with her at all times now. Elgaros sat nearby on a spread of blankets, watching her. Though she hated having her back to him, it could not always be avoided. Rhin leaned over the fire to peer into the pot. Tangled black hair fell around her face as heat washed over her. Green flecks dotted the pasty, gray-brown porridge. It smelled of little and tasted of the same.

Scales rustled behind her, and Rhin pivoted towards the dragon, drawing steel. The movement sent tines of hot pain across her stitched wounds. Elgaros froze, halfway down onto his belly. He bared his fangs, snarling, and unsheathed ebony claws where he still could.

The dragon's golden gaze drifted from Rhin to her sword, then to the porridge dripping from her spoon. "I was only lying down."

"Sorry." Rhin eased her sword back into its scabbard. "S'almost ready. I'll get some honey, make it more palatable."

"It could not be *less* palatable."

Rhin dropped the spoon into the pot, and went to the supply crates near the fire. She wasn't sure how long the garrison's supplies would hold with the dragon here. Scowling, she dug out a jar of honey and peered inside. It was hardened, crystallized, but nothing warmth couldn't solve. She carried the jar back and set it near the flames.

Elgaros watched her the whole time, claws out.

"I hate when he stares at me."

"How else am I to know if you mean me harm?" The dragon flared up his frills. "And it unnerves me when you speak to yourself that way."

"We could talk instead." Rhin swallowed, trying to smile. "Together, I mean."

The dragon arched his neck. "We *are* speaking."

"That's not..." Rhin sighed, rubbing her forehead. After years of her own voice posing as a stranger, even simple conversation was a challenge. "Nevermind."

Rhin scooped half-crystallized honey into the porridge, and stirred it in. Then she ladled most of the pot's contents into an immense wooden bowl. She turned, and held the bowl towards the dragon like a talisman of peace. Steam rose from it in twisting coils.

"I'm bringing your food."

"Very well."

The act was ritual by now. Whether Rhin was bringing food or changing bandages, she always announced her intentions. It kept her from startling him and getting incinerated. She approached the dragon with slow, measured steps. When Elgaros tensed up, spines bristling, she set the bowl atop his blankets.

"I should check your wound." Rhin retreated to the hearth to claim the last of the porridge.

"It hurts," The dragon snarled. "Anything else?"

"Are the stitches holding?" Rhin glanced over her shoulder at the dragon's right forepaw, hidden in bandages. Stitching it up had been nerve-wracking. With every pained hiss, she wondered if the dragon was about to tear her head off. Since then, she swathed it anew each day in fresh, gauzy layers. "If it's not oozing as much, I—"

"Leave it be."

Rhin shrugged and took her food to her favorite chair. The soft maroon cushions covering its pine frame were a boon to her sore body. She unbuckled her sword, then sank into the chair's comfort, sighing. Her wounds still throbbed, but she was used to the pain. Rhin rested her scabbard across her lap, along with her bowl.

They ate in silence. Rhin swallowed a few mouthfuls, scrunching her face. The gruel was little more than ground-up grains she found in storage, cooked in snowmelt and mixed with dried medicinal herbs. She was already sick of it, but the fort had far more grain stockpiled than anything else. Though the honey's sweetness covered the bitterness of the herbs, it could not hide the mushy consistency. She glanced at the dragon to see how he was taking to it. As he licked porridge from the bowl, his ears remained swiveled towards her, but his frills all flattened back in obvious distaste.

"Honey didn't help much, did it?"

Elgaros only grunted, curling his tail. He licked his muzzle as if trying to clear the taste.

"Keeps us alive, at least." Rhin ate another spoonful. "Maybe I shoulda left the bugs in for flavor." She waved her wooden spoon at the dragon. "The herbs will help your pain, fight your fever, and—"

"Must you babble so?" Elgaros snapped his jaws, fangs glinting in the flames. "Your ramblings grate upon my rawest nerve!"

Rhin put her hand on her sword hilt. "Sorry. I'll try to be quiet."

The dragon tilted his head, spiny frills displayed. "Why must you always talk to me?"

"Because I…" Rhin gazed around the room, imagining Echo calling to her from the dark corners and quiet places. "I can't stand the silence, anymore."

"And I can't stand your prattling any more than this slop!" With a frustrated snarl, Elgaros swatted the bowl. It clattered across the floor, splattering gray-brown porridge in its wake.

"Hey!" Rhin shot to her feet, and steel hissed as she drew her sword. "What the hell are you doing, Lizard?"

Elgaros rose just as fast, bandaged paw held up off the floor. "Put your sword away, Murderess!"

"Do you *want* to starve? Or die from infection?" Rhin swung her blade in an arc, tracing the bowl's trajectory. "You've no idea how rare and valuable that is! There's more food and medicine here than I've seen in one place since before—"

"Maybe I'd rather have *fresh* meat than eat another portion of that excrement." Elgaros limped towards her, unsheathed claws clicking against stone. "Put your weapon down before—"

Rhin leveled her sword at his nose. "Back off!"

"The more you babble at me…" Elgaros advanced on her, his tail lashing. "The more I want to—ah!" The dragon gave a sharp cry when he stepped onto his wounded paw. The limb gave out, and Elgaros crumpled. He writhed on the ground, his whole muzzle contorted, tail coiling.

"You brought that on yourself!" Rhin had little room in her heart for sympathy. She fetched the dragon's bowl, shaking it at him. "This could feed me for days! I could survive for years here, if I was alone." She tossed the bowl down. "But I'm *sick* of being alone! So I'll share my refuge, my food, but I will *not* stand here and let you waste it!"

Elgaros eased onto his haunches, clutching the bandaged paw to his chest. He glared at Rhin, panting in pain.

"Do *you* want to be alone, again? Do *you* want to go back to silence and loneliness and wondering if you're the last one alive?" Rhin spun her blade around her hand. "If that's what you want, fine! We can die together, after all. Or maybe one of us survives to eat the other, and lingers alone until the frozen emptiness—"

"I'm sorry." The dragon's voice was a whisper with the strength of a roar.

"Wh-what?"

"I'm sorry I wasted your food." Elgaros licked his nose, gazing at the spilled porridge. His ears and frills all drooped. "That was petulant. I do not wish to fight."

Rhin lowered her sword, still cautious. "Neither do I. But if this is where we're headed, I'd rather just get it over with."

"You spared me. To slay you now would be…wrong." Elgaros curled his tail around his paws, staring down at its spined tip. "Will you accept my apology?"

Rhin wondered if this was some sort of draconic ritual. Was she expected to formally accept and forgive him? "Very well. I accept. Just…" She waved her sword at the gruel spread across the floor. "You have to understand how valuable that is."

The dragon nodded, unable to meet her eyes. "I understand. I will not let it go to waste. When I can hunt again…" He fidgeted with one of his tail spines. "If I find prey, I will share, as you have shared your food."

"I wouldn't turn down fresh meat." She glanced at the dragon's bandages. Wet red stains now marked them. "You're bleeding."

"It is fine." Elgaros clutched his foreleg against his body.

"It's not fine, Dragon. You probably broke your stitches."

"It is *fine*."

Rhin scowled, but swallowed back her anger. Telling him it wouldn't have happened if he'd just eaten what she offered wasn't going to heal his paw any faster. "I'll make you some more food—"

"You need not bother." Elgaros scrunched his muzzle. "I will eat what remains."

"As you wish, but I'm going to have to re-stitch you." Rhin set her sword down on a table, near her chair. "Tell you what, I'll leave this here. If you'd rather kill me than have your stitches fixed, just make it quick." She held her hands up, and gave him a wide berth as she crossed the room to the medical supply crates. "Otherwise, from now on whenever I ask about your paw, be honest."

"Very well." Elgaros gazed at his bandages, muzzle twisting. "It hurts a great deal."

"I'll see what more we have for the pain."

As Rhin dug through the crate, she shook her head, incredulous. *Another day survived.* At least now she had a way to get him talking.

***

Deep in the night, Rhin lay unable to sleep. Her body ached from days of work. Wounds still sore but recently divested of their stitches sent pain spider-webbing across her side. But Rhin was used to pain, and that was not what kept her awake.

It was the silence.

Rhin rolled to her good side, warm beneath stolen blankets. Coals glowed in a small hearth opposite her bed, painting stone walls and wooden dresser alike with a faint orange glow. Her quarters were small, and sparse, nearly identical to dozens of others throughout the fort. When she first returned with the dragon, she selected the room because Elgaros could not fit through the corridor to reach it. But after the first tense weeks had bled into several months of relative peace, what once provided safety now brought only isolation and silent loneliness.

The oppressive quiet reminded Rhin of the day she nearly lost herself. She had traveled the frozen, empty world alone so long that the snow and the silence were the same, cold and smothering. Afraid she would forget how to speak, Rhin just started talking to herself.

One night, sheltering in a cave, her voice echoed back to her. She started asking questions, just to answer the echo. Questions turned to conversations, and before long, she gave her voice a name.

"It's too quiet in here."

"So speak up, Rhin."

"I don't want to hear *my* voice."

Before Rhin met Elgaros, it never bothered her that she talked to herself. After all, Echo was someone to talk to in an empty, dead world. But Echo wasn't *real*. Elgaros was. Rhin sighed, knowing there was no sense denying it. She was used to hearing his voice, now. Without it, she felt lost and alone.

"He's gonna kill you, y'know." Echo's sneer was unfamiliar.

She bolted upright. "That's not funny!"

"It's not a joke! Killing legionnaires is what he *does*. When he doesn't need you—"

"I'm not having this conversation!"

Rhin stood up out of bed and ground her palms into her eyes, shaking. She took a deep breath. *It's only me.* Rhin knew she had to escape the silence. Still in her warm nightclothes, she stepped into her boots, and snatched the commander's blanket off her bed. Rhin stared at her sword as she wrapped the blanket around herself. After a moment's deliberation, she decided to leave the weapon behind.

The corridor outside her room was dark, but she followed the wavering glow of distant firelight back into the grand chamber. Fresh logs blazed in the hearth, and the cold air warmed with every step nearer to the fire. A few days of hard work had transformed the fort's largest room. Rhin covered as much bare stone as she could with animal hides and blankets. They stretched across the floor, and hung along the walls like insulating tapestries. Incense smoldering in bronze censers smothered the musty smells of the fort and the dragon with a spicy aroma.

Elgaros lay near the fire, sprawled across his territory of blankets. Firelight flickered across the bronze blotches dappling his emerald wings. His wedge-shaped head rested on a tattered, indigo cushion as he stared into the fire. A haunted uncertainty drifted behind the dragon's golden eyes. His ears drooped, and his spiny frills trembled.

She froze, her blanket clutched tight. She had never seen him look so lost before. Rhin suddenly felt like an intruder on a very private moment. Just as she was about to leave him to his sorrow, a single green ear swiveled towards her.

"I'm sorry," Rhin said. "I didn't mean to interrupt. Guess you couldn't sleep either, huh?"

"No." Elgaros's voice held none of its usual brassy strength as he lifted his head from the pillow. "I could not."

"Do you want to be alone?"

The dragon sighed. "Your presence is welcome."

Rhin settled into her chair, and watched the fire a while.

"Do humans ever wonder?" Elgaros kneaded at his blanket. "If when you die, you will…see them again? Those you cared for?"

The question caught her off guard, left her tense and trembling deep inside. *Gods, he's grieving.* Rhin scarcely even knew how to answer that. "I know there's people I hope to see again, at least."

"I, too, hope to see someone once more. The ice claimed her, long ago." The dragon took a shuddering breath, his eyes gleaming wet in the flickering firelight. "When I came here, I was ready to die. I thought if I let go, perhaps I'd see her again. I'd been so cold for so long that a little warmth and comfort at the end was all I wanted. But lying here, alongside this fire? I don't think she would want me to die."

Rhin's throat tightened and she swallowed back a growing lump. "Neither do I. I think we owe it to those we miss to survive as long as we can."

Elgaros stared at the red, puffy scars on either side of his right forepaw, blinking away tears. Now that the outer wounds were closed, Rhin let him go without bandages, but the bones and muscles were still healing, and could not yet support his weight. "Then, perhaps we help each other survive a little longer."

"I think that's what they'd want." Rhin leaned her head back, closing her eyes. "Do you…do you mind if I sleep out here? I don't want to go back to that room, and be alone again."

"I would not refuse a night's companionship."

"Thank you." Rhin got comfortable in her chair, swaddled in her blanket.

"You are welcome." Elgaros let out a slow sigh, eyelids drooping. "I think I am for sleep now."

Rhin only smiled. "Good night."

She pulled her blankets up, and listened a dragon's breathing until it lulled her into peaceful slumber.

***

"Be wary, Rhin, and stay near me. There is treacherous ice, ahead."

"Stay close to the big, heavy dragon when we reach the thin ice." Rhin glanced down at the frozen lake beneath her fur-lined boots. "Got it."

Rhin shaded her eyes, gazing up. The wispy clouds revealed hints of the sky beyond, a beautiful sapphire expanse wrapped in gauze. The sun shone as a yellow-white halo, yet brought little warmth to the air. Her nose was numb, and her sinuses ached. At least the rest of her was warm. In the many months that ebbed away while Elgaros worked to rehabilitate himself, Rhin had turned many of the old commander's trophy pelts into clothes, gloves and boots. She offered to do the same for Elgaros, but thus far he showed no interest.

"How's your paw holding up?"

"It aches no more than usual." The dragon lifted his front leg, licking at his scar. "The cold is more unpleasant than the wound."

"May I see it?"

Elgaros extended his foreleg towards her, and Rhin cupped his paw, gently examining it. It was as healed now as it would ever be. Though he could no longer unsheathe those claws, his digits had regained good blood flow. After a few months spent learning to walk anew upon his damaged forepaw, it bore the dragon's weight enough to support him. The scars marring it had faded to fat, pink blotches.

"You sure you don't want me to make you some mittens? I could—"

Elgaros yanked his leg back. "Dragons do not wear mittens!"

"But you'd look adorable in little fur booties!"

The dragon curled his neck to glare at her. His spines were up but his muzzle twitched with the hint of a smile. "I will bury you in this snow and leave you here."

"You'd miss my cooking." Rhin only laughed. "But making *playful* threats? We'll call that progress. What are we looking for, anyway?"

"Be patient." The dragon splayed his ears, a gesture she'd come to recognize as smug amusement. He strode across the ice, tail swishing. "We are nearly there."

Though Rhin wasn't sure why Elgaros brought her to the vast ice field they traversed, the place was beautiful. They walked amidst wind-sculpted snow drifts that stretched in long, snaking lines, as tall as she was. It was like wandering ancient canyons carved in delicate alabaster. Winding granite ledges followed an old shoreline, hemming in the ice. Near the stone, bits of dead vegetation poked through. A thorny branch shrouded in dead moss, a cypress limb clinging to brittle, brown needles and grasping for a warm sun it could never reach.

"What is this place?"

"Used to be a marsh, fed by hot springs." Elgaros waved his paw at a place where frozen ripples and boils marked the ice with abstract sculptures. Further away, wispy clouds of steam drifted. "A few still reach the surface, so stay near the rocks."

As they left the drifts behind, Rhin gazed across the frozen wetland. Wafting steam left dead trees and gray cliffs caked in glittering crystalline sheets. Nearer where the hottest water bubbled up, the ice formed uneven, rounded stairs where heat and cold fought an endless war of melt and freeze. In another place, the skeletal remains of wooden docks and ruined boats jutted from the ice. Glimpses of thatched reed poked from rounded snowdrifts. Rhin's heart sank when she realized there must be a whole fishing village there, buried in the snow. She saw no sign of the crimson ribbons used to mark gravesites in the years following the world's end.

"First freeze musta got them all at once."

Elgaros draped a wing across her back. "Come. This will cheer you up."

Rhin soon spotted something angular and pointed jutting from the snow and ice. Her breath caught as she neared it. "Is that...?"

"Go and see."

Rhin crouched down and drew her knife. She chipped away at the frigid surface until it was clear the object was a broken antler. With growing excitement, she chiseled deeper, exposing dark fur. She brushed trembling fingers across it, then gazed up at the dragon, heart pounding and mouth agape. "Is that...is that a caribou? Did you find a gods-damned caribou?"

"Better." A grin parted the dragon's muzzle, his bronze-edged frills on full, happy display. "I found a *herd* of gods-damned caribou."

"A *herd!*" Rhin squealed the word like a giddy child. She leapt to her feet, and before she could stop herself, she hugged Elgaros tightly around his neck. "You magnificent scaly bastard!"

"Yes, I *am* magnificent." Elgaros patted her back with his scarred paw. "You may unhand me now."

"Sorry." Rhin eased away, beaming. She was far too filled with joy for any embarrassment to creep in. "Where are the rest of them?"

"Everywhere!" Excitement bubbled up in the dragon's voice despite his growled efforts to constrain it. "There's hundreds trapped in the ice. I circled this place the other day, trying to convince myself it was real."

"Hundreds?" Giddy laughter spilled from Rhin. "That could feed us for years!"

"I know." The dragon laughed with her, a happy, brassy bellow.

"Think they came down here during the last thaw? Too many on the ice, and they all went through?"

"I care not, so long as we can eat them."

"Agreed." Rhin rubbed her gloved hands. "We'll bring tools from the fort. I don't want you hurting your paw trying to dig them out."

"You'd prefer I hurt it with some human implement?" Elgaros tilted his head, ears splayed. "Perhaps it's easier if I eat you instead of the elk."

"You *must* be happy if you're trying to make jokes." Smiling, Rhin trotted down the ice field, outpacing the dragon. In her head, she counted every reindeer she saw.

"No jokes." Elgaros padded after her. "Merely wondering why I should keep you around, now that I'm healed and I've found food."

"Because you're going to need my help digging these—"

Rhin plunged through the ice.

There was no warning *crack*. There was no moment of sudden fear and no time to turn back. The ice just gave way in a single, horrifying instant. In that same moment, Rhin was colder than she ever imagined possible. Her body went rigid, every muscle frozen in shock. Icy knives cut her to the bone. Even her panicked mind refused to function properly.

When she felt the bottom beneath her boots, Rhin forced herself to look up. The water's chill was agony in her eyes, but the surface was just above her. Light streamed through broken ice. She could almost reach it, but her sodden clothes were an anchor. Rhin struggled to kick off her boots, to divest her cloak, but numb limbs refused to comply.

The light dimmed. Her lungs ached, and her heart pounded, the only part of her not paralyzed. In a detached, half-conscious moment, she wondered if the cold would kill her before she drowned. The light dimmed further. Something obscured it, tearing through the ice.

Elgaros.

The dragon's head plunged into the water, and Rhin struggled to lift her leaden arms to him. Teeth sank into her cloak, her clothes, and lifted her from the bottom. Claws snatched at her next. Fresh pain cut through the numbness when his teeth and claws went too deep, but Rhin did not resist. She lacked even the strength to help pull herself from the water.

When she broke the surface, she hung limp from his grasp. Cold air struck her, a hammer of ice that left her shattered. Unable even to cry out, Rhin broke into a wracking cough. She spat up water, and wheezed for breath. Frigid air pushed needles into her lungs. The dragon called out, but his voice was distant, garbled, as though she were still underwater.

Rhin blinked, and she was flying. The ground hurtled by beneath her in a white blur. She couldn't even remember being picked up. Elgaros's forelegs clutched her around her middle, and Rhin clung to their warmth.

So cold.

So tired.

In the distance, she heard her name.

"Rhin! Stay awake! Rhin!"

So cold. So tired.

She closed her eyes. His voice went silent. The world went dark.

Movement stirred her to half-consciousness. Rhin lay on stone, her body heaving. Someone turned her head as she vomited cold water. Sharp claws scraped her skin, tore away her clothes. She hardly noticed the pain. Then sudden, unbearable heat consumed her, as though she were being boiled alive. Rhin screamed, thrashing,

"I'm sorry, I'm sorry!" Elgaros's voice sounded unfamiliar. Even as his words settled in, their meaning scarcely registered. "I have to get you warm!"

The dragon pushed her deeper into the hot spring, and with another scream, Rhin returned to darkness.

When Rhin next awoke, everything was blurry and unfamiliar. Strange textures pressed against her bare skin, some soft, others pebbly. Flames painted the world in flickering, red-gold shades. Breath by breath, the fog smothering her mind dissipated. She realized she was back in the fort, lying nude on fur blankets near the hearth. Something green edged her vision.

The last thing she remembered was the joy of seeing so many

caribou, and then…

"Ice." The word came out as a strangled croak.

"You're alright, Rhin." Elgaros's voice reverberated through her. "You're alright, now." Rhin realized Elgaros was curled around her, holding her against his chest. "But you have to stay warm."

Never had she been so close to the dragon since the day she nearly cut his throat. The proximity left her tense. Rhin sucked in a breath, heart thumping. But the fear was gone in a flash, and Rhin knew she had nothing more to fear from him.

"You…" Her voice trembled.

"Don't talk." Elgaros cradled her in his forelegs, encompassing as much of her as he could. "Save your strength."

Rhin gave his forepaw a silent, thankful squeeze.

The dragon replied with a soft rumble, gazing down at her. His golden eyes shone worried in the firelight. "Go back to sleep, Rhin." Elgaros laid his head down and curled tighter around her. "I'll keep you warm."

***

After a day in the cold chopping firewood, Rhin ached everywhere. The snow fell so heavily it looked as though the snowstorm had dissolved all of existence beyond the frozen pine forest. Rhin followed her own half-filled footprints back home until at last the sight of the fort looming through the snow brought welcome relief. She ascended the stone stairs carefully, wary of their icy slickness. Beyond the blue door, wavering orange light at the end of the long corridor promised lasting warmth.

Rhin hurried down the hall with her last load of wood for the day. When she reached the grand chamber, the snow clinging to her cloak was already melting. An immense fire roared in the hearth, painting the room's insulating furs in bright, dancing hues. Rhin tossed her cargo onto the pile she built throughout the day, sending a few logs rolling across the floor. She shook the remaining snow off her fox-pelt cloak and tossed it over a chair.

"The end of the world can kiss my ass!"

"Oh?" Elgaros sat with his wings spread before the hearth. Firelight glimmered on their bronze blotches. "Stopped snowing, has it?"

"Shove it under your tail, El." Rhin peeled off her gloves, then hung her coat up on a hook, grimacing. Her old scars throbbed. "I'm not in the mood for whatever wit you think you've developed."

"And *I'm* not sure that's enough wood."

"Then *you* go get some." Rhin tugged on a boot, hopping around till it came off. "I've been out there six times today, I'm done! We've more than enough wood for tonight. So unless you want this hurled at your head?" She waggled her boot. "You'll shut your sarcastic snout."

"But I wish a larger fire."

"Then get off your ass and help!" Rhin heaved her boot at the dragon.

Elgaros ducked, glancing at the boot as it bounced off a wall. "You know I can't fit through that door. And the main gate's blocked by a drift."

Rhin removed her other boot. "So unblock it."

"I can't go out there." Elgaros arched his neck. "I'm cold-blooded. I'll go into a torpor and die."

"Oh, shut up. You're not cold-blooded, you damn liar. You're warmer than I am!" Rhin took off her snow breeches and draped them near the fire. "You're just lazy."

"No, I just don't want to go out in the snow." Elgaros scratched his neck with a wingtip talon. "There's an important difference."

"Too bad." Stripped to her long, warm underclothes, Rhin joined the dragon alongside the hearth. "Tomorrow, you're clearing that drift and gathering wood!"

"Oh, very well."

Rhin inspected her sore hands. Her olive skin looked orange in the firelight, but she saw no sign of new blisters from the day's work.

"How's your paw?"

"Hurts." Elgaros gazed down at his forepaw. He flexed his toes, then hissed and pinned his spines back. "It's worst when it snows the heaviest."

"I know the feeling." Though Rhin's wounds were long-healed, exertion and snowfall still left her old scars aching. "Let me see."

Elgaros lifted his forepaw, turning it over, and Rhin grasped it. The mottled pink and gray pads were warm and soft. Rhin kneaded the dragon's center pad with her thumbs, working around the fat pink scar. Elgaros grimaced, but the tension ebbed out of his limb.

"How's that?"

"Better." The dragon bowed his head, frills perked. "Thank you."

"My pleasure. Let me check blood flow to your fingers." She squeezed the end of each digit until the pads went pale, then released them. Each regained its color swiftly. "They all look good."

"I've had no such problems for ages, Rhin."

"I know." Rhin patted his paw. "Sometimes I just like reminding myself you're alright."

"That is…" Elgaros licked his muzzle, glancing away. "Kind of you. I am also heartened that you're not maimed or dead." He turned his golden gaze back to her. "Do you wish food now?"

Rhin chuckled, smiling. "That'd be lovely, Lizard."

"Call me that again, Murderess, and you shall go without." Elgaros pulled his paw back, snorting as he rose.

As the dragon limped across the expansive room to the chamber serving as their pantry, Rhin retrieved a bottle of red wine. She hoped a drink would help his pain. If Elgaros was still limping come morning, Rhin would fetch their firewood on her own again. While she waited for him to return, she opened the bottle and savored the aromas of plums and cherries before she set it aside. A pang of nostalgia struck her, along with a memory of picking cherries in a village orchard with her mother. The image warmed her even more than the fire.

"I've good news and bad news." Elgaros's voice preceded him

before he dragged in a half-frozen reindeer haunch. "The good news is you won't starve. The bad news is—"

"It's caribou again?"

"Yes." The dragon glared at her, as if offended she'd ruined his poor joke. "I think the *real* bad news is that I have to keep putting up with you." He cocked his head. "You know, after all your wretched gruel, I should imagine you'd be overjoyed to have eaten caribou for six months." He gestured at the reindeer leg. "Is this enough?"

"More than."

Rhin rubbed her forehead. *Had it really been that long?* She'd never done well with time, let alone in the absence of definable seasons. But if Elgaros was right, then by now a year must have passed since they first drew each other's blood, only to choose to share survival instead. Rhin sighed, deciding it didn't matter how long it had been. Each day survived was its own victory.

Elgaros set the haunch down in front of the hearth, licking blood from his muzzle. "There is only one more left before we must dig another from the ice."

A shiver racked Rhin. Though they'd returned and retrieved caribou safely many times now, that moment still left her shaken. She rubbed her arms, suddenly chilly. "We could consider braving the valley too, try for something fresher."

"There are treacherous things dwelling there. It is a large risk to take when we still have food available, but I am willing if you prefer it."

"Thanks." Rhin hugged the dragon's neck, stroking his scales. "We'll play it by ear."

Elgaros patted her arm. "You are welcome. But I still do not understand that expression. Do humans often play games with their ears?"

"Good question." Rhin released him, then fetched her knife. She crouched, sliced off a few strips of meat, and stood back up. "The rest is yours."

"If you insist." The dragon settled onto his belly. He clutched the frozen caribou between his front legs and licked at it like a hound with a treat.

Rhin chuckled and shook her head. "If a dragon could ever be adorable…"

"Hrrm?" Elgaros glanced up, jaws parted. Blood coated his snout and dripped from his sharp teeth.

"Nevermind." Rhin laughed and threaded the caribou onto a skewer. When she set it over the flames, the meat hissed and sizzled. "Bring me your drinking bowl, I'll get you some wine."

Elgaros rose and stretched his neck to the shelf holding his belongings. He plucked the oversized wooden vessel in his jaws and dropped it at Rhin's feet. Rhin crouched and poured him most of the bottle. Immediately, Elgaros shoved his muzzle into his bowl, noisily lapping.

"No need to sip it," Rhin said, emptying the bottle into her own mug. "We've got more."

Elgaros licked red droplets from his pebbly scales. "Your sarcasm would be more effective if we did not, in fact, have more."

Rhin glanced at the boxes of drink stacked along a wall. Though they'd emptied a few, plenty remained. "Old Commander Ice Corpse must have been a real lush."

The dragon cocked his head. "A lush what?"

"A lush. You know, a real lush."

"Repeating it does not make the meaning clearer."

"It means a drunkard." Rhin sipped her wine, relishing the ripe fruit taste. "Someone who drinks too much."

The dragon lapped up a few more mouthfuls. "You're describing yourself."

"Says the one with wine running down his snout."

Elgaros snorted. "Your food's on fire."

"What?" Rhin spun around. Her skewer lay in the hearth. "Son of a bitch!" She dragged it out of the fire with the poker. "Damn it, now it's burned."

"Everything you eat is burned."

"That's called cooking, Dragon."

"Then enjoy your charred ashes."

Rhin let the meat cool while she fetched her favorite chair. It sat near the small bed she dragged into the grand chamber not long after Elgaros saved her from the ice. These days, she was far more comfortable sleeping near him than alone in an isolated room. Rhin moved her chair over to the dragon, then piled the meat from her skewer onto a wooden plate. She flopped into her maroon-cushioned seat with a long, weary sigh.

"Gods, it's nice to sit down. Feel like I've been hauling wood all day." She shot the dragon a glare. "For some reason."

Elgaros flattened his frills, glancing at the fire. "I'll gather more wood, tomorrow."

"Don't worry about it." Rhin nudged the dragon with her foot. "How's the wine?"

Elgaros licked his muzzle, rumbling a throaty purr. "Quite enjoyable. Wine is one thing humans got right."

"We got plenty right." Rhin popped a bite of meat into her mouth, making a face. At least the char gave it an unfamiliar flavor.

"Such as?"

"Ale." Rhin leaned her head back, sighing. "Ale was great."

"Was it better than wine?" Elgaros licked his bowl clean.

"Just as good. And you can drink more without falling over. Maybe we'll find a barrel someday." Rhin smiled at the dragon. "I'd love to share some with you."

"I would also enjoy sharing the only other thing humans got right."

"We got more right!" Rhin laughed, gesturing with her mug. "We invented society!"

"Did not." Elgaros waved a paw dismissively. "Dragons had clans long before we fought you."

"So? We created whole civilizations!"

"And oppression."

Rhin scowled, swirling her cup. "Don't act like dragons weren't out there conquering villages."

"That's different." Elgaros laughed, a halting, growling sound. "Regardless, ending the world nullifies any good your people accomplished."

"We did *not* end the world!" Rhin shook her head, sharing his laughter.

"Well, it wasn't me." Elgaros smiled, frills perking up. "That just leaves you."

"Yes, it was my doing, all along." Rhin stood up, taking a mock bow. "I ended the world."

"At least you admit it."

Rhin finished off her food and set her plate aside. "I'm going to take a hot bath. You should come too. Soaking your paw will help."

Elgaros tilted his head, his voice softening. "Are you inviting me to bathe with you?"

"It's too quiet down there without you." They were rarely apart, anymore. The longer they survived together, the lonelier Rhin felt when she couldn't hear his voice. She rubbed her arm, shifting her weight. "It reminds me of...how I almost lost myself, when I was alone."

The dragon rose to his feet, and stretched his neck to gently nuzzle Rhin's cheek. "You're not alone, anymore."

Rhin smiled. Elgaros's growing affection lately was warm comfort, a balm for her soul. She cupped his muzzle in her hands and stroked his scales, earning a coarse but happy purr. "Neither are you. Come on, we can soak our scars together."

***

"Do you wish me to look away while you undress?" Elgaros sat on his haunches, half submerged.

Rhin shook her head. Between her daily proximity to the dragon, and being rescued from the frozen marsh, modesty was a distant concern. "Nah, you're fine."

Their tub was a hot spring that bubbled up in the fort's back chamber. In ages past, someone carved the bedrock around the spring, creating a deep, squarish pool. Time wore its edges smooth. Ancient sigils were cut in the wall above it, speckled with blue-green algae. Coils of steam drifted aimlessly away from the hot water until they escaped through ice-caked fissures in the stone.

Rhin stripped off her clothes and laid them near her flickering lantern. The warm steam kept the air from feeling too frigid against her bare skin. Rhin draped a towel alongside the sunken tub. She sat down on it, dipping her feet in the hot water.

The dragon cocked his head, watching her. "You look good without your clothes."

"Didn't know we'd been stuck together *that* long." Rhin laughed, ears warming. She didn't mind the way he stared, anymore. "But thank you just the same."

"I was complimenting your health. I cannot see your bones anymore."

Rhin examined her wavering reflection in the lamp-lit water. Her olive skin shone in the lantern's glow. Elgaros was right. Her ribs no longer showed themselves. "Barely even look like I survived the apocalypse. We might be sick of caribou, but—"

"Better than your porridge."

Laughing, Rhin slipped off the edge and eased into the water. The heat made her suck in a breath. As her body adjusted, she settled across from Elgaros, and stretched her legs to get comfortable. One foot bumped scales, and the other brushed the inside of Elgaros's hind leg, then something softer.

"Hey!" Elgaros's ears shot up.

"Sorry!" Rhin giggled. "Is that one of your—"

"Yes!" The dragon grunted, squirming. His frills flushed dark.

Rhin rarely saw the dragon embarrassed, and couldn't pass up the chance to further it. "So should I move my foot, or wiggle my toes?"

Elgaros gave an odd, whining growl. He glanced away, licking his muzzle. "You'd better not."

Rhin only laughed. "Better not what, this?" She wiggled her toes.

"Uurrrn! You're going to…" The dragon shifted, rustling his wings.

"Are you enjoying this?" Rhin eased her foot higher, waggling it. "I didn't think humans—"

"How long do you think it's been since—" Elgaros cut himself off with a snap of his jaws, spines flared. They drooped back down just as fast. "Foolish question."

"Sorry. Cruel joke." Rhin braced her foot against his hind leg, instead. "Better?"

"It is less intimate." Elgaros flattened his ears.

"I can't tell if you're relieved or disappointed."

The dragon rustled his wings, sloshing water. "Neither can I." He peered down at her, head tilted. "Are you not embarrassed?"

Rhin shrugged, then dunked her head, considering the question. She popped up and wrung her hair. "What's left to be embarrassed about? It's just us, and this frozen world, El."

Elgaros murmured, scratching at his jawline.

"Besides, the look on your face was priceless."

"Oh, get mounted."

"You'd never fit." Rhin laughed and splashed the dragon.

"Hilarious." Elgaros lifted his left forepaw from the water.

"Aw, shit—"

Elgaros smacked his whole front leg against the surface. Rhin threw her hands up as an immense wave crashed over her. It sloshed out of the tub and across the floor. Sputtering, she wiped water from her eyes, shaking her head.

"Truce, truce!"

"No truce!" Elgaros lifted his paw higher, his neck arched. "Proclaim your surrender or I launch a second assault!"

"Fine, fine!" Rhin tried to smack his paw away. "I surrender!"

"Then I declare victory over the Murderess Empire!" Growling laughter, Elgaros tapped her nose with a single finger pad, claw retracted. "A truly great day for dragons everywhere."

"Get your damn paw outta my face!" Rhin pushed the dragon's foreleg away, but savored the sound of brassy dragon laughter rolling between stone walls. "See, this is why I like having you down here with me."

Elgaros tilted his head, ears splayed. "You enjoy being splashed?"

"No, the sound!" Rhin waved a hand around them. "The echoes."

"I thought you hated echoes?"

"I hate *my* echo." Rhin cringed, and glanced away. "But when you're here, laughing with me?" Her smile returned, and she reached up to stroke Elgaros's jaw. "It's like there's dozens of people, talking and laughing *with* us."

The dragon's ears swiveled to follow the fading sounds. "That is a pleasant thought."

Rhin leaned back against the warm stone, rubbing her arms. "You know, before I met you, I hadn't heard another voice in years. It was just Echo and me."

"So I've heard." Elgaros stretched a foreleg to touch her shoulder.

She shivered, her voice trembling. "Did I tell you I started calling myself Rhin?"

Elgaros drew his head back, sucking in a breath. "Isn't that your name?"

"Some days I wasn't sure." Rhin faltered, dragging her fingers through her wet hair. "Whatever slow, insidious madness I had spiraled into, it was your voice that pulled me out of it." She smiled up at him, taking his paw between her hands. "But sometimes I wonder if it's truly Rhin you saved at all." She took a shuddering breath, glancing away. "Or if Rhin was already gone. When I'm alone, and all I can hear is my own voice, I start to wonder if I'm just the echo."

"It matters not who you were, Rhin." Concern shone in Elgaros's golden eyes. He stretched a dripping wing open in invitation. "All that matters now is that you are my friend. You are…" The dragon trailed off, then swallowed. "Important to me."

Fighting back a sudden lump in her throat, Rhin sloshed through the tub to hug as much of the dragon as she could. "Thank you." She stroked his scales, leaning her head against him. "You're important to me, too."

"I am glad." A smile crossed Elgaros's muzzle, but ghosts drifted behind his eyes. "When you went through that ice, I felt like my heart went with you." The dragon's spines trembled, his wings tensed. "That was when I realized you were becoming something more, to me. Not just a means to survival, but a reason *to* survive." The dragon paused for a few breaths. Hoarseness crept into his voice when he spoke again. "I knew in that moment that I would save you, or die with you. I would *not* go back to being alone."

"Gods, El…" Rhin leaned her head against his scales, and the dragon enclosed her in the sheltering warmth of his wing. She stroked his chest plates, smiling. "As strange as it sounds, waking up alongside the fire with you curled around me? After all those years alone in the cold, it's a wonderful memory. I smile whenever I think of it."

"As do I." Elgaros cleared his throat with a growl. "Imagine what your people would think, hearing you say such."

Rhin chuckled, bittersweet. "My people are dead. My mother would have understood, but the rest? Probably clap me in irons. Taboo just to be friends with a dragon, let alone cuddle with one, or…" She glanced up at his face. "Whatever you consider us. What about your people?"

The dragon snorted, tossing his head. "I would be scorned, at best."

"I'd say we bear our black marks together, but there's no one left to judge us." Rhin stroked his emerald chest plates. "Even if I still tell myself there are other survivors."

"Perhaps there are. When the next thaw comes, we can try to cross the southern mountains again. If we find anyone, we can bring them here."

Rhin poked his shoulder. "Maybe we'll even find you a female dragon."

"I would not object to being cradled under someone's wing again." A wistful smile parted Elgaros's muzzle. "Kalyvir and I used to hold each other that way." His ears drooped, and he lifted a paw to wipe his golden eyes. "I miss her, sometimes."

Rhin cringed inwardly. They had talked now and then about lost loved ones, but tried not to stir up painful memories in one another. She stroked his neck. "I miss Bear, too."

Elgaros arched into her touch. "I still find that an odd name for a human."

"A childhood nickname. He was sighting on a bear with a drawn bow, trying to act brave, but his buddy startled him and he let fly. The bear charged him and he ran, only for the bear to drop just at his heels. Turned out, his shot hit an artery. Everyone in our village called him Bear ever since." Rhin smiled, shaking her head. "Kinda funny, since he was so scrawny. But he had a big heart and an infectious laugh. After we grew up, we saw each other a few times a year. At night we'd just lie in bed, by the hearth, talking about old times."

"That sounds pleasant." Elgaros curled his wings around himself. "Kalyvir and I also spent many nights sharing pleasure and companionship. We'd watch the stars, cradled in each other's wings."

"I'd have never guessed dragons were so tender." Rhin smiled. "It sounds lovely."

"It was."

"I miss that sort of thing." She gestured with a dripping hand. "Gentle touch, being held, lying alongside someone."

Elgaros made a sound like a rattling, murmuring whine. "I also miss these things." He lifted a paw to scratch around a horn. "If you wish, I would not be adverse to…"

As he trailed off, Rhin looked up. "Yes?"

"We could lie together."

Rhin giggled. "I don't think that's quite what you meant."

"Shush." The dragon splayed his frills. "I was only offering to hold you." Elgaros's tail curled against her leg, scales brushing skin. "If we ever wish to have these gentle comforts again…" The dragon slapped his paw against the water's surface, huffing. "Nevermind. It is a foolish idea."

"No, it isn't." Rhin took his paw in her hands. "You're right. There's no one left to hold us but each other."

Elgaros nodded once, gazing down at her. "Last time, I was afraid you would not wake. It would be pleasant to hold you again without fear."

Rhin gave the dragon's scar a kiss, then smiled at him. "I'd like that, El."

***

"This may work best if you lay down first." Rhin surveyed the grand hall, still nude but wrapped tightly in her favorite blanket. Thanks to the extra wood she loaded into the hearth before their bath, the room was warm. "Then I can settle next to you and get comfortable."

"Very well. Allow me to prepare a space for us."

Rhin stepped back to let Elgaros clear some room. First the dragon moved her bed aside, and collected all the blankets from it. Elgaros spread all her blankets on the floor alongside his own, in front of the fireplace. Recently, Rhin had sown large furs together to make a blanket big enough for Elgaros to cover himself with while he slept.

Elgaros eased onto his belly, then rolled to his side. He draped his wings behind him, and kicked his hind legs out across the floor. "Is this position acceptable? My underside should be warmest for you."

"That's fine. Do you mind if skip my bedclothes?" Rhin fidgeted with her blanket. "You're almost as warm as the fire. I don't want to overheat."

"You will not be uncomfortable lying naked with a dragon?"

"I wasn't." Rhin laughed and dropped her blanket, savoring the fire's heat on bare skin. "Till you put it that way."

The dragon stared at her, his head tilted. "You need not feel embarrassed. You look quite beautiful in the firelight."

"Thank you." Rhin smiled, blushing.

Rhin retrieved a pillow, and sat down upon the soft bedding, scooting up against the dragon. The segmented plates protecting his chest gave way to pebbly scales across his belly. Towards his hind end, the scales grew finer. Rhin eased her back up against him, and found his textures and warmth pleasant.

Muscles rolled under Elgaros's scales as he draped a foreleg across her stomach. "How is this?"

Rhin set her hand on his, staring at her olive skin against his green scales. "Quite nice, actually. You?"

"Enjoyable enough to pretend you didn't try to slay me."

Rhin brushed her fingers over the broader scutes across the front of his foreleg. "You started it."

"You were in a Legion cloak, investigating Legion wagons. I assumed you were hunting me."

"You *assumed* I'd be delicious." Laughing, Rhin caressed the back of the dragon's forepaw.

"That too. Luckily for you, you make better company than dinner." The dragon lifted his head, gazing down at her. "Your touch is pleasant."

"So is yours." Rhin twined her fingers through his. She laid her head on her pillow, eyelids drooping. "This is lovely."

Elgaros curled, enclosing her in his sheltering warmth. "There are more blankets, if you become cold."

"Thank you." Rhin squeezed his paw. "I'm just going to enjoy this, a little while."

Between warm comfort and the fatigue of a hard day's work, it was not long before Rhin struggled to keep her eyes open. As slumber's gentle waves lapped across her mind, she did not resist. Before she knew it, Elgaros was scooping her up in a foreleg and carrying her against his chest.

"What are you…?" Her drowsy voice was only a murmur.

"You were asleep." Elgaros laid her down in her bed. He draped her blanket across her. "I thought you would be more comfortable sleeping here."

Rhin reached for his paw, squeezing it. "Thank you."

"Good night, Rhin."

***

The next few weeks fell into a simple, comforting rhythm. They gathered wood, lounged alongside the fire, bathed, and then lay together at night, talking. They rationed their food to make it last until the heaviest of the snows abated. Each day, Rhin found herself looking forward to that evening a little more. Whenever she lay against Elgaros, she felt at peace. Every night, she let his voice lull her to sleep, and each time he carried her back to her bed.

When night next fell and Rhin was once more lying against the dragon's belly, she squeezed his paw. "I've been thinking about what you said about the mountains."

Elgaros lay his limb across her midsection. "What about them?"

"That we should try to cross them again." Rhin rubbed the scutes protecting his foreleg. "If there are other survivors…"

"The winds through the passes are only safe during the thaws, and the clouds are too cold if we venture any higher. Miss that opportunity, and we will be forced to turn back, as before."

Rhin nodded, tracing a circle on the back of his forepaw. "I think we owe it to ourselves to try."

"It is difficult to predict a thaw, so we should prepare in advance." He lifted his head, gazing down at her hand upon his scales. His ears were splayed, his frills half up. "May I touch you? As…you are touching me?"

"Of course," Rhin said, smiling. When Elgaros's fingers brushed her arm, Rhin lifted it to give him more room. "This might be easier."

Elgaros nodded, resting his paw against her side. His pads were warm, and softened by all the time spent walking on animal furs. As he stroked her awhile, Rhin savored his touch. Soon, his paw drifted across her hip, and down her leg. Rhin shivered, arching her back. That was as intimate a touch as he'd ever offered. Not since before the freeze had she known such tenderness.

"You are quite soft."

Rhin chuckled, knowing Elgaros meant it as a genuine compliment. "I suppose female dragons aren't so soft."

"They have softer places."

"So do I."

The dragon's paw froze on her hip. "I…I should stop."

"Sorry. Been ages for either of us, huh?" Rhin set her hand atop his, looking up at him. His frills were flattened, and confusion whirled in his golden eyes. "You can keep going. If it helps, I'm enjoying this."

"I fear if I continue I may…" Elgaros looked away, lowering his voice. "Unsheathe."

"Is that what dragons call it?" She glanced towards his hind end. "When they get hard?"

"Yes." Elgaros's frills flushed purple. "It would be embarrassing."

"Oh, come on, Lizard, it can't be *that* small."

Elgaros gasped, his spines flared. "It is *not* small!" He laughed, hissing at her. "That is a cruel blow, Murderess."

"Made you laugh, though." Rhin clasped his paw between her hands. "I promise I won't be offended."

Elgaros kneaded his other forepaw against a blanket, crumpling it. "That is kind, but it is quite wrong to be so displayed in front of a human."

"We talked about this, El." She twined her fingers through his, sighing. "There's no one left to judge us."

The dragon gave her a long, thoughtful look, his ears half-splayed. "You are right. I shall cover myself, if need be."

"Don't. It's alright." Rhin leaned her head against him. "Honest question. Are you uncomfortable with this?"

The dragon arched his neck. "Embarrassed, but not uncomfortable. Are you?"

"No." The ease and certainty of the answer surprised her. "If anything, I'm enjoying myself." She chewed her lip, thinking about it. "This is our life now. I don't want to spend the rest of my days never knowing tenderness or being touched that way again. You said before that I was important to you, but you're important to me too, El." Rhin kissed his paw before returning it to her hip. "I'm comfortable wherever this leads. I'll leave it up to you."

Elgaros lifted his paw, and it trembled slightly. *He's more nervous than I am.* Anticipation twisted her belly while his touch hovered just above her skin. His pads brushed her hip and slipped down to her knee. Rhin pressed into his touch as his paw glided up the back of her thigh, to her rump. His caress made her shiver.

"I like your haunches." The dragon's paw roamed in a slow circle.

Rhin relished the feeling too much to reply. At the dragon's gentle coaxing, she parted her legs. His touch along her inner thigh left her warm and tingling. Elgaros traced a single finger up and down from her knee to her crotch. The pebbly scales of his foreleg brushed over her skin, ruffled her soft pubic hair. Rhin murmured her enjoyment, watching his hand wander.

"Where do humans like to be touched before mating?"

"I like to be kissed, all down my neck." Rhin took the dragon's paw, and guided it to her right breast. "With a hand here. Be gentle, though."

"Always, Rhin."

When the dragon cupped her breast, the encompassing warmth made her gasp. With her guidance, Elgaros massaged it in a slow circle. Rhin moaned as his pads rubbed her hardened nipple. Attuned to the sound, the dragon shifted his grasp to tease only a single finger's pad around the bud in lazy motions.

Rhin's moan turned to a whimper. "That's nice, El…"

"I should like to kiss you now, as dragons do."

She sat up, and Elgaros curled his head down to lick her throat. The heat of his tongue made her gasp. It was almost too hot. He cupped her breast again, massaging it. Rhin put her hands over his, panting. The heat of his tongue roaming down her neck left her squirming and rubbing her thighs together.

Rhin leaned over to kiss his scales. Any lingering hesitation ebbed away breath by breath. It didn't matter that he was a dragon. They weren't enemies, anymore, they weren't human and dragon. They were just two survivors, with a connection growing deeper by the day.

"May I let my tongue wander?" Elgaros's touch drifted downwards, and a single finger pad teased the folds between her legs. "Here?"

She sucked in a startled, excited breath. Till then, she wasn't sure how far they'd go. "That sounds wonderful." She glanced down at the dragon's hind end. One back leg lay further forward than the other, obscuring what rested between them. "Are you...what did you call it?"

"Unsheathed. And yes."

Smiling, Rhin kissed the softest part of his nose. "Show me first?"

"As you wish, Rhin."

The dragon withdrew his concealing limb and cocked it in the air to expose himself. The thick green sheath normally slung between his hind legs was retracted, allowing the dragon's penis to jut out. Unlike a man's, it was deep crimson and tapered from thick, ridged base to pointed tip. A minor flare sat behind its point like a spearhead. The whole thing was faintly arched. Behind it, the dragon's testicles were snug from excitement, oval shapes silhouetted against the green skin.

"That looks as dangerous as the rest of you." Rhin laughed and shook her head. "Not sure I'd know where to begin."

"I shall accept that as a compliment." Elgaros rolled back towards his belly, nuzzling her bare skin. "May I continue?"

Rhin cupped his muzzle and gave his nose another kiss. "Absolutely."

Elgaros licked her all down her throat, and Rhin could not imagine a more tender gesture for a dragon. Soon he nuzzled a breast, then swirled his tongue across it. Rhin gasped, arching her back. The sensations of scales and tongue so close together were almost too much to bear. He repeated the act a few times for each breast, and each time Rhin moaned.

As scales brushed and tongue writhed, Elgaros's pads trailed up her thigh, leaving goosebumps in their wake. The closer his touch drew to her womanhood, the further Rhin parted her legs. When he reached her body, he teased her sex with a single finger, gliding against her entrance. Shuddering, she stroked his foreleg.

Rhin eased onto her back when the dragon pushed his muzzle between her legs. She drew her feet up and rested them against the sides of his neck, her knees parted. Elgaros licked each thigh, closer and closer to her body. When the wet heat of his tongue flicked across her folds, Rhin whimpered and bucked her hips in silent plea for more than just a tease. That tongue parted her petals and slid inside.

His sheer heat made her gasp. "Oh, gods!"

It was almost too hot. *Almost.* Rhin squeezed her thighs around his snout, soft scales rubbing delicate skin. The dragon curled his tongue, stroking it over inner walls. Rhin moaned, only for Elgaros to withdraw and swirl his tongue against her outer lips. Just as quick, he plunged it back inside and twisted it. Rhin cried out, rocking her hips.

Elgaros slipped his forepaws under her rump, hoisting her. As he worked his tongue, Rhin squeezed her breasts, wriggling in delight. The dragon lapped at her, each lick parting her around his tongue. When it found her clit, Rhin arched her back, grinding against his muzzle.

"There! Right there!"

In response, Elgaros gave a playful growl, the vibrations permeating his tongue as it circled her nub. Rhin grasped at the blankets, squirming in bliss. Elgaros alternated his movements, seemingly searching out what drew the loudest cries. Sometimes his tongue roamed deeper, curling inside her. Other times he spent long moments working it against her outer folds, or rolling its tip against her clit.

Rhin thrust herself against his muzzle, happy to let her reactions guide him. As her pleasure grew, she sat up to stroke his nose. His golden eyes lifted and locked with hers. Once more, his tongue wiggled her sensitive bud. Sweet pleasure rolled through her. She caressed his scales, encouraging him.

"Yes, right there! Don't stop!"

Elgaros's tongue danced around her clit in frantic rhythm. Such hot, constant stimulation was almost more than she could take. The blissful friction grew into a ceaseless tide of delight threatening to carry her way. Breathless, Rhin pressed to him, the last few seconds lingering like hours.

At last, Rhin threw her head back and screamed as ecstasy clenched her inside and out. She squeezed her eyes shut, writhing against his muzzle. The dragon's tongue swirled and twisted all through her orgasm. Only when she flopped back onto the blankets, limp and panting, did he slow. The dragon gave her a few final, tender licks, then lifted his head, smiling.

"I am pleased you enjoyed yourself."

"Oh, g   ods, El." Rhin ran her hands down her face, trying to catch her breath. "That's an understatement. Thank you…"

"You are welcome." Elgaros sat up, still quite erect.

Once Rhin's breathing eased, her gaze settled between his hind legs. "Patient, isn't it?"

Elgaros glanced down at himself, licking his muzzle. "Starved for affection better describes it. It will soon retreat."

"The hell it will." Rhin laughed as she got to her feet. "Can you lie on your back?"

As Rhin went to dig through supply crates, she peered back at Elgaros. The dragon eased onto his back, wings draped at his sides, crimson erection displayed across his emerald underbelly. "I dunno how you've kept that thing hidden."

"Carefully. It is…unseemly to be unsheathed in front of

humans." Elgaros looked away, embarrassment darkening his frills.

"Well, you needn't hide it anymore." Rhin found the jar she sought, and returned to the dragon. "This is warming oil for aches and pains, but Bear and I used it for something else. Unseemly or not, I'd like to use it on you."

"That does sound pleasant. Go ahead."

Rhin settled herself against the underside of the dragon's tail, near his body. The warm, pebbly scales teased her skin. She set the jar aside, and ran her hands down Elgaros's thighs, towards the dragon's testicles. Her fingers brushed his scrotum and it tightened, outlining the treasures within. Elgaros arched his neck, watching her.

When he offered no objection, Rhin slipped her hands under the dragon's balls. They were heavy, a pleasant weight overflowing her palms. She rolled them around, exploring their shape. They were ovoid, like a man's, only far larger. Their pouch lacked scales, just soft, smooth skin. Rhin gently massaged one plump egg in each hand. Elgaros gave a little cooing moan.

Smiling, Rhin opened the jar and dipped her fingers into the oil. She rubbed her hands together, then cupped the dragon's balls again. Rhin rolled each dragon testicle between both hands, working slick oil into emerald skin. Elgaros murmured, his spined tail-tip curling. Soon his sac glistened, relaxing again in the newfound warmth.

"How's that?" The oil left Rhin's skin warm and tingling. "Not too hot?"

"No." Elgaros took a slow breath. "It's nice…"

"Good." Rhin dipped her fingers back into the jar. "It's limited, so if we do this again, we'll try the tub."

With fresh oil on her fingers, Rhin wrapped her hands around the end of the dragon's maleness. It was as hard as any man's, and far hotter. She gave its pointed tip a few slow, tender strokes, just past the spearhead flare. Elgaros whimpered. His eyes were half-lidded, and his tongue peeked from his maw.

Rhin worked lower, rubbing him between her hands. She scooped more oil, spreading it across his sensitive red skin. When her palms slid over the raised ridges around his thick base, Elgaros trilled, pushing himself into her grasp. Rhin traced the little creases with her fingers, and the dragon shuddered, hind paws splayed.

Once he was nice and slick, Rhin stroked him with both hands. Her palms glided against his flesh with ease. Elgaros trilled again and lifted his hips, his length sliding through her fingers. Savoring his pleasure, she pumped the dragon with long, slow motions, working his whole shaft.

The dragon's paws curled, and his voice shuddered. "That is…b-blissful!"

Rhin smiled. There was something disarmingly sweet about a creature so powerful reveling in such intimate pleasure. She twined one hand around his pointed tip, and twisted it down against his flare. When it made the dragon gasp, Rhin repeated it. Elgaros wriggled and squirmed, hind paws flexing. He thrust into her grasp. Rhin held him that way, and let him drive himself through her fingers a while. Though she suspected he was trying to be gentle, the force of the dragon's motions still rocked her back and forth. As he humped at her hand, Rhin played with his balls, massaging them.

When the dragon's breathing increased, Rhin leaned forward. Cradling his maleness, she lifted it away from his belly, and brushed her lips against it. Rhin kissed it all down its underside, earning delighted whimpers. The oil gave him a faintly bittersweet taste. At its base, Rhin kissed each ridge. She squeezed his tip, and pumped it swift and steady. A little burst of hot liquid spilled over her fingers, and the dragon groaned.

Rhin smiled at him, fingers dancing. "Getting close?"

Rhin climbed across the dragon, breasts brushing scales. Once in position, she eased back to straddle his length and trap it between their bodies. Elgaros shuddered. Cupping his tip in her hand, Rhin lifted him and pressed her heat to his, rolling her hips. The dragon gave a reverberating groan, paws clenched. He clutched his forelegs to his chest as if he dared not touch her for fear of harming her in his exuberance.

Slow at first, Rhin rubbed herself against him in sinuous motions. She held the end of him in her hands, stroking in time with her movements. Elgaros's tip dribbled, and she worked the slick fluid down till her hands met her body. When she ground her hips in lazy circles over his ridges, she pumped him again. The dragon's responding thrust lifted her whole body. Rhin decided it was safest not to try and take any of him inside her, in case he grew too forceful in his delighted distraction.

Elgaros's head lolled as his moans grew louder. Rhin used his rise and fall to help stroke the softest parts of her body against him, moving faster. She pumped him harder, stimulating as much as she could. The dragon's balls tightened under her, and soon he was gasping and panting.

"Ah!" Elgaros's muzzle scrunched up, his ears back. "Please don't stop!"

Rhin pressed harder to him, trapping as much of his erection between their bodies as possible. She rocked against it, grinding her sex across him, her buttocks rolling over his ridges. Her palms were still slick with oil, and they glided up and down his last few inches in smooth motions.

"Aaahh! Rhin! I'm…I'm—"

Elgaros clamped his jaws shut, muffling a roar as his body tensed and his back arched. His hips rose, lifting Rhin with them. All his spiny frills shot to full extension, bronze edges unveiled in an expression of draconic bliss. His maleness jumped against her, and a thick whitish burst splattered his belly scales. A second, larger spurt marked his chest, then another. Elgaros twisted, tail coiling and hind paws curling. Rhin kept moving, kept his pleasure going till he finally went limp beneath her.

As the dragon lay panting, Rhin eased herself off him. She settled against his hind leg, and stroked his scales while he basked in the afterglow. When Elgaros finally lifted his head, she smiled up at him.

"Thank you, Rhin. That was…exceedingly satisfying."

Rhin couldn't help but laugh at the way Elgaros put it. "Glad to hear it." She got to her feet, and fetched a towel to wipe him down with. "When you catch your breath, let's go wash up."

In the hot spring, Rhin helped scrub his scales. When they were both clean, they returned to the grand chamber. She put a new log on the fire, and snuggled against the dragon's chest. Elgaros curled his foreleg over her. Something about the gesture felt more meaningful now. He held her closer than before. For a while, she simply savored his warmth and presence.

"I am happy we found a reason to keep surviving, Rhin."

"Me too." Rhin wove her fingers through his. "I think I'd like to sleep here tonight, with you."

"I would like that." Elgaros curled around her, purring. "Sleep well, Murderess."

"Good night, Lizard."

As Rhin slipped into slumber's comforting waters, a strange sense of peace settled over her. Wherever their lives led next, she was glad to have Elgaros with her.

Outside, the snow fell in silence.

***

"Are you sure about this, Rhin?"

"That's the third time you've asked." Rhin cinched the last of many packs stuffed with supplies against the dragon. He was as loaded as could be without impeding his flight.

"If we cross those mountains, and the thaw dissipates, we may not be able to return."

Rhin gazed up at the sky. It was as clear and blue as she had ever seen it. The sun brought rare warmth to the air, a fiery eye reflected in blinding glare against the endless white. Fog drifted across the distant lowlands, and clouds swirled around the tallest peaks hemming in the valley. To the south, the mountains were lower, with wider passes, a natural gateway to a warmer land. At least, it was warmer once.

"Are you sure you saw wings, El?"

Elgaros gazed to the south, his frills flattened. "It was difficult to say, through the clouds and at such distance…but yes."

"Then I'm sure, too." Rhin climbed up onto the dragon's back, settling at the base of his neck. She knotted her safety rope around her middle, patted Elgaros, and took a deep breath. "If there's anyone left out there, we'll find them. Let's go."

Together, they ascended towards the sun.

SUPERNATURAL DELIGHT

Whyte Yoté

Levi was never so relieved to take an off-ramp. Every mile had seen taillights and street lamps brighten as his super night vision had kicked in. To top it off, he could now hear every supersonic squeak and engine noise, and there were plenty.

With a trembling and increasingly hairy hand he turned off his headlights and coasted into the almost-deserted parking lot of a rest area somewhere south of Moline, Illinois. He'd tried to make it further—even halfway between Moline and his frat in Monmouth would have sufficed—but the vertigo and nausea WebMD had told him to expect forced him to cut it short. Nowhere near as bad as last month, when the change had overtaken him for the first time, but still torture. Back then he hadn't made the connection until the moon rose over the horizon, much too late to formulate a coherent plan in his addled brain. He still didn't know what he had done that night.

The past month had not been kind to Levi Fettwandler. So when the urge to leave town grew too strong, a morbid sense of relief replaced the seemingly ever-present dread he'd felt for weeks. He wanted—no, *needed*—to get away. Not anywhere in particular, just… not urban. That he'd skipped out in the middle of his cousin's bat mitzvah would have to wait until the crisis passed, and he was pretty sure coming out as lycanthropic would gain at least a few sympathy points. At least he'd never heard his family badmouthing weres in his presence.

He saw one other vehicle, an SUV with a horse trailer attached, so naturally he parked as far away as he could. Idly Levi wondered if the trailer was for full-time horses or just part-time horses. By the time he managed to get out of the car, his clothes felt so suffocating that it was all he could do to not rip them apart. Now slightly itchy all over, he folded everything neatly on the back seat and took the keys with him until he realized he no longer possessed pockets. The tailpipe proved too hot, so Levi tucked them into a rear wheel, and began to run.

Less than a minute later, he fell against a tree, out of breath. He hadn't done any serious running since high school and it showed. His "freshman fifteen" had turned into at least fifty, and electrical engineering wasn't exactly the most athletic of courses of study.

Taking stock against the bole, Levi tried to remember what little he'd read: not curable but managed by various suppression methods, usually took up to three days per month, the resultant species random and unpredictable. All very easy statements to make by the unafflicted, and cold comfort to someone consciously undergoing his first real change. Looking down his round belly, Levi studied his right foot, watching the bone structure of his toes lengthen, the nails narrowing to claws.

It wasn't painful, which was a surprise. He'd read that it could be painful depending on the person, and fully expected at least a little excruciation. But it was just the itch, and the weirdest sense of his body developing in ways that put puberty to shame. Not only that, but also he wanted more than anything to find out what he'd actually turn into, since he'd blacked out last time. He still couldn't remember what had happened that night, but no one had turned up murdered or anything so he figured he was safe on that account. Reports were super-rare anyway, and not in the United States for at least a couple decades.

Who knew transformation would go mainstream? Still, given the choice, Levi would rather have never contracted it in the first place. Wrong place, wrong time, and one very inattentive technician, who was hopefully out of a job by now.

Levi's nose began to push out, the end turning black, whiskers popping out of his cheeks. The changes started to accelerate, his growing feet throwing him off-balance. Anxiety welled up from deep within his chest, but rather than succumb to a panic attack, he forced himself to breathe slowly. Each breath brought a little respite even as he listened to his larynx shift. He didn't dare open his eyes; not losing consciousness held more priority over watching.

He'd have the rest of his life to watch, anyway, provided science couldn't find a cure.

When he couldn't stand on his shifting legs he fell back onto the dried leaves and opened his eyes. The moon stared down at him with indifference, catching his eyes and locking him as if by tractor beam. Replacing the itching, a rush of warm euphoria flooded his body. He counted out the next five minutes second by second as he let the change finish its work. Once he felt sure he was out of the woods, he opened his eyes and looked down.

"Oh, shit."

***

The moon was still high in the sky when Levi noticed the flickering glint about a quarter mile off, leading him to believe midnight hadn't yet arrived. By that time he'd gotten used to walking on his toes, along with a little help from some conscious tail-swaying. His head had begun to swim shortly after the end of the transformation, and now his stomach rumbled almost constantly. If he didn't eat something by the end of the night, he might not make it back to humanity.

He'd heard horror stories of weres discovered half-formed when they had died mid-change. There were the ones taken off-guard by their first time and unaware of the need for protein to get back. There were the ones who wanted to hunt instead of driving to the nearest McDonald's for several dozen McNuggets, and never found prey. And there were those done with it all and purposefully starved themselves so the change would kill them without all the mess.

So when he saw the orange-yellow glow dancing through the trees, hope and desperation picked up his pace. Shoving away thoughts of ill-intentioned hunters (or even just the careless ones), he instead pictured a bonfire with food and water, welcoming any who might stumble into that part of the woods. Complete bullshit, but Levi needed something to carry him. The alternative simply wasn't an option.

As he grew closer, several voices rose above the night cacophony, the words unintelligible but the laughter clear. At a hundred feet he slowed; at fifty he lifted his feet higher and carefully sidestepped dry twigs and leaves.

At forty-one feet, his world turned upside-down.

Levi didn't hear the *thwack* of the rope tightening around his ankle, but he heard himself yelp as he went ass-over-teakettle into the air. The abrupt silence from the camp, followed by cheers, terrified him. Even from this distance he could hear them getting up, slapping each other on the back, and one guy even peed on the fire before catching up to his buddies. Levi's new hearing caught it all, but the jumble of different footsteps proved impossible to nail down.

He frantically tried to reach up to untie his ankle, but the transformation had done exactly jack squat for his chubby nerd body. He couldn't bend that far right-side-up, never mind fight gravity's effects on his…everything. Plus the added weight from all that extra fur. Gasping for breath, he gave up and waited for his fate. As the footsteps came ever closer, he did the only thing he could think of: shut his eyes tight and wait for it all to be over.

"What do you think it is?" asked one particularly mincing voice, high-pitched and youthful.

"You're not gonna believe it," said another with a slight country drawl.

"You've got to be kiddin' me," added the third, butter-smooth, a slightly younger Bing Crosby.

The steps slowed as they closed the last twenty feet. "Cliff, shine your phone," said the young guy. Levi's eyelids exploded into a curtain of veiny orange.

"That's what I thought," said Bing, whose name was apparently Cliff.

"Told you," the country boy repeated. "Smelled him as soon as we left the campfire. Gotta admit, I'm a mite disappointed. I was hoping for a snack to go with my beer."

Realizing he might not be doomed after all, Levi opened his eyes to slits. The phone's LED cast enough light that he could clearly see a bloodhound, a hawk, and…a four-legged hippopotamus, who caught him looking and grinned before tramping over. Warm nostril air flowed over Levi's newly-fuzzy face. "Sorry hon. Jack over there's a carnivore and likes to trap things." The dog was shirtless in a pair of overalls, the hawk clad in cargo shorts and a leather vest, and the hippo was starkers. Naturally.

"Yeah," Jack said, "but no poodles. I don't cannibalize my own species, no matter how ugly the breed."

Levi felt his hackles rise, surprised to find himself bristling a bit.

Cliff scoffed. "You're a part-time dog every month, and suddenly you're proud of 'your' species?"

"I've been doing it long enough, yeah," defended the bloodhound. "What's it matter, anyway?"

"It doesn't," said the hippo. "Can we just get the poor thing down? He's miserable. By the way, I'm Aidan."

Relief washed over the poodle. Cliff loosened the knot and Jack lowered him to the ground as the hippo watched. They helped him get to his feet, steady if not a little wobbly. Once the blood drained from his head, he cleared his throat. "Uh…if you're not gonna eat me, can I at least warm up by the fire?"

Cliff chuckled, the creamy feathers on his bare chest fluttering. "I think we owe it to him after all that rigmarole. Whaddya say, boys?" They agreed, and soon the poodle had a cadre making sure he didn't stumble his way back.

Not only did they take him to the firepit (which turned out to be more of a campsite, though Levi could see only one large tent), but also Jack fetched a blanket for the naked poodle and Cliff whipped up some quick Swiss Miss complete with tiny marshmallows. Lacking opposable thumbs, Aidan lay next to the relit fire and offered moral support. As he sipped, Levi realized that none of his "captors" had remarked on his nudity and gave silent thanks.

The quartet sat in silence for a good several minutes; the ice broken by Levi's capture rapidly solidifying again.

Cliff was the first to speak. "So. I guess we should start with names since we basically have all night. You know ours by now, so pipe up." The hawk had an authoritarian air about him, but with an undercurrent of warmth that almost seemed paternal.

"Levi," said the poodle, licking his lips. "This is really good."

"It's the fake chocolate, so you won't get sick." Levi gave the hawk a quizzical look. "Bromine? Bad for dogs?"

When the poodle shook his head, Cliff nodded. Jack and Aidan traded knowing looks.

"It's your first time, isn't it?" asked the bloodhound, sending a flush of warmth up into Levi's face. He felt stupid for acting like a complete noob, but these three put him at a massive disadvantage.

"Second, actually. I don't remember the first."

Aidan stood and trod over to the poodle. "You went savage, huh? I'd hug you, but…yeah." He waggled a thick foot. "In any case, I'm sorry. Sometimes that happens."

"If you're wanting to jaw to some sympathetic ears," Jack said while popping a can of Coors with a claw, "you've stumbled to the right place. As you can see, we're all in the same boat." The fire drew wild purple shadows over their features, giving everything a slightly sinister hue. But now that he knew he wasn't dinner, Levi let himself really relax for the first time that evening. It felt good, and his anxiety faded to a mere whisper. He was among friends, and friends were exactly what he needed right now. "We've got all night. Why don't you start off and tell us how you got fuzzy in the first place."

"Dialysis." Levi was surprised how quickly and easily the word escaped his lips, even though it did hitch a little at the end. Jack swore under his breath. Cliff just shook his head, and Aidan gently nuzzled the poodle's hip.

Raising the can to his lips, Jack said, "That's a new one to me. It's also a damn shame." He took a swig and belched, puffing his jowls a bit. A clasp came loose but the bloodhound ignored it.

"But how?" Aidan asked, lying back down. "They have measures in place for stuff like that."

Levi shrugged. "Doesn't matter anyway. Nothing I can do about it."

"I'm sure you can sue the pants off 'em." The hawk leaned back against the fallen log on which Levi sat, gazing into the flames. "At least, I hope you're going after them."

"I'm trying, but there's a lot of red tape. I can't even prove it happened at the treatment place. I go three times a week and I didn't turn right away. Just, the next full moon after…that was it." How he was able to hold back the tears escaped him. "I'd have to track down the source and match the DNA, and *that* doesn't even prove it. I could've gotten it anywhere, according to them."

Aidan scowled. "Or from anyone. There's still the sex stigma, especially in 'alternative' circles." Levi knew exactly what the hippo meant. "I'm lucky; my mom's boyfriend turned me when he got a little too angry and just bit my arm." His tone turned bitter. "She's still with him. That's why I left. These guys saved me too." He nodded toward the others, who were both pointedly looking away.

Levi asked, "Aren't wereferals pretty rare?"

"Yeah, it's not the easiest thing." The hippo smiled all the way up to his ears. "Wanna know a secret?"

"Sure."

"When I'm not a hippo, I'm a ninety-nine pound twink. Can you believe it? How weird is that?"

"Lord works in mysterious ways," opined the hawk without looking up.

"Oh, that's nothin'," Jack piped up, gesturing with his can. "Get this: me 'n a buddy are out huntin', okay? Couple years ago. Looking for a buck, something at least twenty points, and my bud—Charlie's his name—spots a goddamned *bear* about fifty yards away. He says, 'Jacob, I'm gonna take that fucker down and put his head up on my living-room wall!' Before I can say jack shit, he's runnin' off, and bam! Bear's down. He asks me to help him dress the thing, and sure, why not? Never dressed a bear before."

The poodle noticed Cliff rolling his eyes. Apparently he'd heard it before.

The bloodhound continued unabated. "So we get in there, and I'm slicin' some meat off the ribs when the damn knife slides on some gristle and tears my thumb wide open. Month later I wake up in a cold sweat with my face pushed halfway out and my tail almost broke from layin' on it. Didn't make the connection until I remembered that was the last time I injured myself."

"So the bear wasn't really a bear?" Levi asked.

"Doesn't behoove you to think about it too much," Cliff interjected, stepping forward to grasp a piece of firewood in his shiny sharp talons before tossing it onto the flames. "We all know the implications, and we don't need to entertain them any more than we have to. Already done it too much myself."

"He never did get around to the taxidermist," said Jake.

Aidan made a face. "Ew. Can we move on? Once was enough, back when I joined."

"And I don't think Levi will mind, will he?" the hawk asked with a pointed sideways glance.

"No, you can go ahead."

"Good." Clearing his throat, Cliff said, "On a lighter note, my wife and I were just about to turn our fostering skills into parenting skills when it happened. We were all set to adopt one of our foster boys when our newest little girl turned the second night we had her."

Levi grimaced. "Jeez."

"And attacked the rest of us."

"Jeez!"

Cliff smiled a sad smile. "Fortunately we were able to barricade the rest of the kids in a back bathroom until help could arrive. They ended up tranquilizing the batty thing, but not until she'd covered us two in bites and scratches. And, well, that's about it."

"I've got nothing on you guys, that's for sure."

"When you get down to it," Cliff said, "it's tragic no matter what you do. You're story's no better or worse than ours. Same result, right?"

Silence united them in agreement.

Levi couldn't see how these guys could keep so positive in the face of so much adversity. Then again, these guys were the first and only shifters he knew of, and he knew precious little of lycanthropy to begin with. The internet went only so far.

"So you couldn't adopt?" he ventured at the risk of opening old wounds. The hawk's smile never faltered.

"Not after the blood tests came back," said Cliff. "One of us, maybe. Both of us, no chance. Three days a month with a sitter for foster kids?"

Levi nodded in sympathy. That wouldn't fly with authorities even in the most liberal of cities.

"So we fell back upon our degrees because we had to. We do alright, but it's not what we would've wanted."

"Hopefully you won't have to make many big changes, Levi," added Aidan. "It's kind of 'luck of the draw' there. At least you're still on two legs."

The poodle grinned. "I guess so. Funny you should say that. So far my kidneys seem to be improving. I'm still debating whether to tell my doctor or not."

"Sooner or later," said Cliff, "somebody's going to notice

something on a test result, and you'll have a lot of medical personnel on your back. Tell the doc now and avoid a panic later. Especially if you're doing bloodwork. They may even be able to hook you up with some suppressants if you end up hating it." The hawk had a point.

"That regeneration stuff is pretty great, isn't it, kid?" Jake threw his empty beer can into the fire, where it sizzled, and stood to pad over to the poodle. Without warning he unfastened his one remaining shoulder strap and the dirt-stained coveralls fell to the ground, leaving him in just his fur. Bending over Levi, he pointed to the center of his breastbone. "Take a gander, as close as you want. I had open-heart surgery about eight years ago, and can you see a scar?"

The poodle shook his head, fighting to keep his eyes forward instead of down. It took some effort, which in itself disconcerted him. And he'd be damned if he didn't feel a familiar twitch between his legs which, in his present company, was even more disconcerting. Only so much could be contributed to anxiety or excitement.

"Darn right you can't," Jack continued, going so far as to pull apart the fur where the scar was supposed to be. When he pulled away he kicked the overalls off his foot and went back to sit on the log across from Levi. The other two seemed unaffected by the bloodhound's nudity, but the poodle found his eyes constantly darting in Jake's direction and had to consciously turn away his head. "In fact, *my* doc said it was probably the best thing to happen to me. Not only is my heart improving, but my liver's back to normal too!"

Cliff said, "He thinks he's out of the woods if he only drinks during the full moon. He may be right, actually. His progress's been nothin' short of stunning."

"Countin' on it. I used to be an alcoholic, pretty close to cirrhosis. Then I found out this furry thing kind of counteracts that stuff. I don't get drunk like I used to, I only do it a few days a month, and my liver's better than ever! So I guess you could say this 'curse' as some people call it is a blessing for me."

For the first time Levi could see a sliver of light at the end of the tunnel. Eventually he may not have to set foot in a dialysis center again for the rest of his life.

"So." The hawk leaned back and crossed his arms. "We found you naked in the woods with a yarmulke on your head. The obvious is easy to guess, but would you mind filling us in on the rest of it?"

Jake and Aidan waited patiently on the other side of the fire.

"Well, I was hoping last month was a fluke, so I made the mistake of not canceling on my cousin's bat mitzvah. I didn't want to back out, since I try to be a *mensch*. Yesterday I could feel it, but didn't want to believe it. It got so bad that I had to leave in the middle of the Hora."

The others looked at him quizzically.

"The chair dance."

"Oh," they replied in chorus.

"So I drove as far as I could, pulled off and ran into the woods, and got caught by you."

Aidan yawned. "It's a good thing you did, probably. You seem a lot calmer now."

The poodle was just about to argue the fact when he realized the hippo's assessment wasn't far from the truth. Aside from a slightly fast pulse and an annoying restlessness in his legs, the panicky anxiety that had brought him out here had all but faded.

"I don't know," Jake said. "Would you call that calm, or tense?" He nodded in the poodle's direction, where Levi realized he was scratching at his balls, and quickly withdrew his palm.

To his horror, an inch of bright red protruded from the sheath he hadn't even touched yet. He hadn't needed to. Now he stared at it, studying the way the curly charcoal hair (or fur, he might have to do a little research on that) bunched up like pubic hair, how it thinned out and became finer as he felt past his sac and lower…

"You tryin' to give us a show?"

Levi's head flew up, his paw pressed flat against his groin. Unfortunately (for the poodle) he only succeeded in skinning back another couple inches between his fingers. His gasp wasn't unexpected but his subsequent moan was. All three males looked at him with more than passing interest, and Levi found himself reciprocating with a mixture of horror and desire.

Aidan came over and plunked down next to the poodle. "You're feeling funny, aren't you? Like, you never have before." Levi nodded weakly, and the hippo gave a sympathetic nudge.

"One thing they don't really report on is how lycanthropy can also change your preferences," said Cliff as easily as if he were reading a weather report instead of giving potentially life-changing news. "Looks like you're at least bi, if not full-on gay." And the hawk shrugged.

Instead of being upset, Levi could only manage mild despair. So far, his first conscious foray into furrydom hadn't turned out to be the existential crisis he'd expected. Before midnight he'd made three friendly acquaintances, been fed non-deadly cocoa and warmed his bare ass by the fire. What was a little craving for cock? He laughed louder than he meant to. "Sorry. Just a lot to take in. Does it go back to normal when I...you know."

"I don't really know what counts as normal anymore, especially when it comes to bein' horny for somebody," Jake said, pulling on his own semi-hard sheath. "But yes, it does, at least for me. I'm straight as they come the rest of the month, but right now you couldn't make me hard for a chick if you tried. Right now I'm bein' a lecherous old fart but I don't care. You got a nice body, son."

Levi blushed. But he didn't move to cover up. He didn't want to. Lecherous old fart or no, he liked the attention.

"Same here," Cliff said. "Usually straight, but...I guess you could say I'm one of those trisexuals."

"You'll try anything once?"

"Most anything. I guess you could say I was bi until Aidan showed up." It was the hippo's turn to blush, made super cute by the dainty way he carried his bulk. The implications needed no introduction.

"Guilty," Aidan admitted. "And I'm queer full-time. My big change was only in the body department."

"So you two have…?"

"Oh my, yes." Cliff pushed off from the log and began to shrug off his vest. "All three of us, actually. That's the main reason we meet here every month, aside from the company and common struggle."

Levi had to think about the phraseology of his next question. "Not to pry, but how do you and your wife handle…you know."

With a slight chuckle, Cliff replied, "Depends on the month. I don't come to the group all the time. Sometimes we just stay inside with the kids and have a movie night. Nothing's different except they have a dadbird and momcat. Their names, not my idea."

"They're cute." The poodle smiled.

"Not only that, but we also want to let them see it's not a disability, and we can go to the mall without being asked a million questions. We still get stared at," the hawk admitted, "but that's human nature."

The poodle's disbelief melted away into arousal tinged with envy. He joined the bloodhound and hippo in watching the hawk strip his svelte feathery body. Without wings in the way, Cliff made quick work of his clothes, which he folded neatly on the log before sitting again. This time he couldn't cross his legs for obvious reasons…or he just wanted to show off the nine inches of tapered shaft over a large set of downy balls. Lycanthropy had been especially kind to him.

I want to put that in my mouth, thought Levi, further horrifying himself, before he noticed the change in the air. A subtle shift of scent into something heavier, more substantial. More potent. He was fairly certain their little pow wow would eventually evolve into some kind of intimate party at the very least. Suddenly he felt their eyes on him, more appraising than judgmental. They were sizing him up, and he was reciprocating.

Cliff's a hunk, no question. I almost hope he picks me. Jake is nice in a 'good ol' boy' kind of way, with lots of experience. And Aidan…well, he makes a damn cute hippopotamus. I guess if I were hot enough for it…

"Talk about gettin' into the spirit of things," he heard Jake say, followed by a low-pitched wolf whistle. "You ain't too bad yourself."

The bloodhound cupped his own balls, rolling them around in his paw before tugging his sheath down a bit more.

Levi ogled the show for a few seconds, realizing he was just as hard as Jake. He looked down to see a good seven inches of shaft sticking out of its curly-furred home. A couple more inches of knot remained hidden, but not for long. "I have a girlfriend," he said as if describing a bowl of pea soup.

"Aidan has a boyfriend," Cliff piped up. "I'm married with two boys and a girl, and Jake is still a confirmed bachelor."

"Yeah, well this fuzzy business is a lot of baggage." Jake shook his jowls to emphasize the point. "Don't want to burden some pretty thing with all of this."

"You can burden me anytime," Levi mumbled before clasping his paws over his muzzle, which had begun to burn anew. Three sets of eyes regarded him. "I didn't mean that."

Jake grinned. "'Course you did. Everybody knows when a politician says some shit and changes the story after the backlash? Usually the first round was the truth." The bloodhound squeezed his knot, turning the head a deep veiny purple. "Nothing wrong with that. You want this cock up your ass, you can have it. That is, if hippobutt over there doesn't want my load first."

Blushing, Aidan studied the ground as he scraped dust this way and that with the bottom of his foot. "Actually..." he started, meeting the poodle's eyes, "I kinda wanted Levi to do that tonight. If he wants to, that is."

"I don't *own* you." Jake sauntered over to pet the hippo between the ears, a hairless tousling. "You can do whatever—and whoever—you want." Apparently, the two had established their own full-moon roles. It was kind of cute. While Levi felt a little like an interloper, his dick seemed open to the idea. *Something* was keeping blood in the thing, at least.

Aidan thanked the bloodhound by nursing him for a couple seconds, then closed his eyes and went on vacation. The sight of hippo lips around a dog dick, while certainly odd, was also a lot more arousing than Levi thought it had a right to be.

"Now that that's settled, we can get down to business?" asked the hawk. "My balls aren't gonna drain themselves." Indeed, Cliff's sac did appear swollen and needy. Levi wondered where that load would end up.

The woods seemed to close in around them, with its not-quite-silence of white noise and insects. Aidan bobbed lazily on the blood-hound with lidded eyes and an expression of contentment that looked right at home on his broad muzzle. Levi watched as Jake brought a paw to the hippo's head, but instead of holding him down with it he started a gentle stroking of one of Aidan's ears in a gesture far more intimate than a simple fuck buddy would use. Aidan hummed and redoubled his efforts.

Levi looked up when something big and pink crept into his periphery. He turned to find himself face-to-tip with Cliff's prodigious cock.

"You okay?" asked the hawk, hands on hips. Musk rolled off him in waves, drowning the poodle in pheromones.

"Yeah," said Levi, though he didn't really believe it. What he felt and what he wanted to do were two very disparate concepts.

Cliff sat down on the log, inches twitching perpendicular to his body, and draped an arm over the poodle's slightly shaky shoulder. He had to clear his throat to get Levi's attention, but he kept smiling nonetheless. In that gentle way. In that *fatherly* way.

A shudder ran through him.

"Still havin' trouble with those emotions, son?" The hand slid down to his side and squeezed enough to make the poodle feel secure but not enough to seem pervy. "We all have to deal with them. Not everyone changes teams either. We all found each other, so we stick together. It's a mite easier than going it alone every month."

Levi nodded, trained on the hawk's equipment but miraculously still paying attention.

"And I can't speak for the guys, but I'm pretty sure you're welcome any full moon."

What happened next surprised everyone, including the poodle. He turned to Cliff, tears ready to spill out onto his curly charcoal fur, but stuck his tongue down the hawk's throat instead.

Ignoring the weird sensation of his jaws clamped down around the edges of the hawk's beak, Levi threw his arms around the puffed-out neck and squeezed. Cliff went stiff and squawked softly into the poodle's muzzle, eventually encasing him in a fatherly hug, first patting his back and then just holding him. Jake and Aidan had probably already noticed, but if they had they'd remained silent. Not long after, Levi pulled back, sniffing.

"Sorry."

"Sorry?" asked the hawk, incredulous. "Boy, you're a hell of a kisser. I mean, I know you're just lettin' off steam but damn. Just damn."

"That did look nice," added Aidan before stuffing his snout back under the bloodhound's low-hangers. "So does that," he continued, muffled.

Levi looked down at the red rocket jutting stiffly from his groin. A drop of moisture glistened at the tip. In human form he'd be lucky to get anything before the finale, but increased libido was one of the possible side effects and more common than others so it made sense. He ran his fist up the length of his shaft, sending the drop on its way. A moment later it was joined by another.

"This okay?" Cliff's fingers merely circled the poodle's flesh without stroking, one small step at a time. The hawk's own member had reached its peak, appearing sharp and angry in the firelight.

Levi nodded, reaching out to run his pads along the tight chest, the narrow torso, the absence of any pudge whatsoever. What came next seemed at once odd and completely natural. "You're so beautiful."

"Flattery'll get you everywhere, son. Would you've said that before your happy accident at the dialysis center?"

The comment gave the poodle pause. He liked Cliff. A lot. And he didn't know why. Maybe it was his mellow, matter-of-fact nature that had disarmed Levi's anxieties. Or his world-wisdom. Certainly it couldn't be the thing around which he could barely circle his fingers. On the other paw, it couldn't hurt.

"No," he said. "Definitely not a guy, much less a bird."

"Of prey, son."

"Yes, sir."

Cliff's gold eyes narrowed to crafty avian slits, accompanied by the pinch of claws on Levi's cock. "What was that?" he asked honestly.

"Nothing," Levi muttered, realizing his mistake which, judging by the scent wafting from the hawk, qualified more as a happy accident.

"Say that again."

The poodle realized his tail had plastered itself to the log in an attempt to tuck between his legs. If not for his erection he might have pissed himself, but new blood surged there instead. He held his breath, avoiding Cliff's predator stare, until the hawk's beak nudged his nosepad.

"Boy?" Who knew Bing Crosby could sound sexy?

Forcing his head up the last few degrees despite beginning to tremble, he mustered the words in a soft whimper. "Yes...sir."

Cliff smiled, at once arousing and terrifying. *This is what mice see right before they're eaten. Or raped. Or both.*

"Cliff? Clifford?" Aidan and Jack had taken another break to move closer to the action. "If you're thinking of doing what I think you're thinking of doing, you can think again."

"You know I wouldn't do anything to hurt the boy. He's just pressin' my buttons, is all. I know the rules. Consent and all blah blah and you've never had a problem with me."

Aidan's expression softened a bit. "Sorry," he said, turning to Levi. "To you, too. I've got some baggage from an ex who was allergic to asking first."

"We all got baggage." Jake stood there, arms crossed, dick dangling, and shrugged. "We can schedule a kaffeeklatch for next month.

73

Right now I need to breed something."

"Dibs on the poodle," Cliff piped up. Levi flushed furiously, venturing a paw behind to still his wagging tail. "Leave it," said the hawk. "It's cute." So much blood rushed to his face and cock at the same time he dropped his jaw to pant, after which he realized "dibs" meant his ass stuffed full of hawk meat. Yet his heart didn't leap in terror. It was more a skipped beat of anticipation.

The hippo nudged Levi's knee. "Is that okay? If Jake takes me first? I know you wanted to."

Levi couldn't believe these words were coming out of a four-legged hippopotamus. Finally throwing the last of his caution to the wind, the poodle bent to plant a kiss between Aidan's nostrils, lending a pink tone to his grey skin. "You're so solicitous. I'll take sloppy seconds. There's always next time."

"You're coming back? You mean it?"

"How can I say no to that face?"

A paw landed on the poodle's shoulder, followed by a hand on the opposite. "Glad to have ya, kid," said Jake.

"Y'already know what I think," Cliff added.

"Speaking of, why don't we get this show on the road?" Jake asked, already maneuvering behind Aidan to line up his cock. Cliff and Levi watched Aidan's face turn from surprised to pained to blissful in a matter of seconds. Hippo and bloodhound sighed in unison.

"I've been waiting all month for this." Jake seemed to speak for Aidan as well. "How's that, kid?"

With a hum and a soft stamping of feet, the hippo murmured, "Heaven." His big flat-toothed maw fell open when the bloodhound's hips began to move, both of them falling into a rhythm not foreign to either.

"Make yourself useful and tend to that thing before it explodes," Cliff suggested to Aidan. A moment later Levi had big rubbery lips nestled in his pubic fur, but before he could even process the sensation (familiar yet new, like everything else about lycanthropy it seemed), the hawk had stepped closer and now smeared musky moisture against the poodle's cheek. "And I'm sure you know what to do."

Levi did know, and he was more than happy to oblige. He only had to turn his head and open wide so the hawk could slide in. Stronger at the base than the tip, the scent filled up the poodle's nose and made his sinuses tingle. The tip tickled his uvula but the familiar gagging sensation never arrived.

"I know the line's overused, but are you sure you've never done this before?" Cliff asked, now adding his hips to the motion of Levi's head. "Won't get me off that way but it's real nice." He extended "real" for a long second.

Jake chuckled while thrusting. "You've always been a hard nut to crack from oral. Sometimes I swear my jaw aches for days, but the trying sure is fun."

"What about Aidan?" asked the poodle around his mouthful of cock.

"Not even Aidan." The bloodhound paused on an in-thrust and the hippo grimaced, then both heaved sighs of relief.

The poodle gawked. "Did you just come?"

"Not yet," said Aidan. "He just likes to shove his knot into places."

"Damn," Levi mused. "That doesn't hurt at all?"

Aidan replied, "Yup, just a little. S'okay, that's what rumpuses are for."

"And Aidan has the best rumpus," Jake said, stating the obvious. As if he needed to prove his point, the bloodhound smacked the hippo on one large round flank, sending a wave through Aidan's body.

"Flaunt it while you got it, honey," replied Aidan, "It'll be gone come morning. Either way, I've got a feeling my consolation rear won't disappoint."

"You're almost predisposed to it, aren't ya son?"

The poodle looked up into Cliff's beak and shuddered. Predisposed? Maybe. But still a virgin in the backside department, giving or receiving. Cliff's tapered shape might be best to start with, but until then…

"I'll…give it the old college try?"

"Bully!" Jake interjected with a horrible British accent and a finger-monocle over one eye. "Stiff upper dick and all that."

Cliff offered a dramatic sigh. "We really need to cut him off sooner in the evening." Then he chuckled in spite of himself. "Oh well. Keep suckin', Levi."

The poodle needed no encouraging, and went right back to work, wondering what he was in for as he bobbed almost involuntarily. Images of himself guiding his cock into Aidan's hole held his attention, turning into images of his tongue deep under Aidan's tail, post-coitus…buried in that hot sweaty—

"Mmmph!" Eyes wide, Aidan swallowed frantically to keep up with Levi's spontaneous orgasm, which overtook him so abruptly he had to pull away from the hawk to avoid biting his dick from the strain.

Levi's world washed away in a roar of blood. It reminded him of his freshman year at Monmouth, doing whippets in his buddy's hot tub. He felt a mild pulsation and figured he'd popped, observing from miles away with an objectivity that both fascinated and terrified him. *So this is what it's like to come without an orgasm.* Aidan was talking but the poodle only caught the end of it.

"—lot! When was the last time you jerked off?" The hippo licked bits of stray cum from the whiskers on his chin. "I mean, I'm not complaining, but jeez! You taste really good, though," he giggled. Hippo giggles were so cute.

Reluctantly, the poodle pulled off Cliff to catch his breath. "Usually…I don't…even come that much."

"Point for lycanthropy," the hawk opined. "I suppose you're out of commission for the remainder?"

"Y'all talk too fuckin' much," grunted Jake before Aidan gave a yelp and his bright baby-blue eyes crossed. "There we go…" The bloodhound ended with a long, drawn-out sigh of deep satisfaction.

"And boom goes the dynamite."

Levi saw the puzzle pieces coming together. He looked down at his own cock with incredulity. "Did he just...?"

"He sure did," Aidan said, seconding Jake's satisfaction. "He still is, actually."

"Guess I'm more dog than you are, son." Somehow when Jake called him that it just wasn't the same.

"Well?" Cliff, hands on plumescent hips, waved his member in the poodle's face.

Levi took a minute to gather himself. Normally he was a one-and-done kind of guy but—as with most everything else related to lycanthropy—things had changed, and for the better. Not only was he ready to go again, but also he felt legitimately anxious...the good kind of anxious. Anticipatorily anxious. "Well...those guys seem busy, but I guess I'm free." He grinned, at ease and relieved for it.

The hawk crossed his arms and returned the grin. "I think you'll fit in perfectly here. We could always use more, if you know what I mean." Levi inferred the double entendre just fine. "You wanna be on your back or over the log?"

Levi paused, unmistakable horror on his face. "You...and me?"

"No, me *in* you."

"Missionary is easier on the knees," Jake said, bringing images of Aidan on his back with all four legs spread.

"But doggy style makes it easy to go deep," countered the hippo.

"Your call, son." There was the shudder again, even stronger than before. Part of him wanted it badly, but another part—probably the human part—was screaming self-preservation. Plus he *really* wanted to fuck that hippo hole.

"Fuck!" Jake sighed and backed up from Aidan's rear, cock softening and retreating. "You should see this back here. Thing of beauty." The hippo blushed again.

Wringing his paws in his lap, the poodle had to tell the truth: "If it's all the same to you, Cliff, could you take a rain check? I don't quite think I'm ready."

Suddenly the hawk squatted in front of the log, balancing with his paws on Levi's knee. Cliff's beak didn't show much in the way of emotion, but his eyes made up the difference. "Hey," he reassured the poodle. "I'm not gonna make you do anything you don't feel like, son."

Giving his sheath a final wipe, Jake said, "You know, Aidan here could probably get on his back and you'd be fine, if you feel like blowing again." He threw Aidan some bedroom eyes. "I've always wanted to see you gettin' fucked all close and personal."

"Never done missionary before," said the hippo. "Well, not like this at least."

"Yeah, fellas, but I'm not giving up that easy," the hawk said good-naturedly. "We just gonna make a poodle sandwich or what?"

He was half-joking, but Jake perked up like it was a good idea. "You know, that's not half-bad. Aidan can suck upside down just fine. He's probably still thirsty anyway."

The hippo stayed quiet, speaking volumes.

"What do you say, kid?" asked the hawk. "Wanna lose a few more cherries before sunrise?"

Levi's face and tail echoed the sentiment.

"Okay, well, you guys get yourselves all squared away and I'll sit here with my dick getting soft." He crossed his arms and waited while Jake helped Aidan onto the log, rolled him onto his back, and teeter-tottered him rump-high.

"That doesn't hurt either?" Levi asked the hippo.

"Nah, thick skin," Aidan said. "Actually it's pretty relaxing."

"Not for long," Jake added. "Get in there, son. Won't find a looser hole this side of a pussy."

Suddenly nervous, Levi took his cock in paw and squeezed again, relishing the spasms it created. He'd never tried anal—never even *suggested* it before with his girlfriend—so he was not prepared for the heat that surrounded his tip, nor for the tightness despite his easy entry. As tempting as it may have been to slurp up the stuff just deposited, his hair trigger from earlier had somewhat tempered his arousal. Goodness knew how long he would last this time.

He knew he should feel weird using another guy's cum as lube, but…it just didn't matter. Compared to everything else, that was relatively tame.

Aidan's thick rear legs twitched as he moaned. "Ohhh Levi, that feels so good." His cock, a prehensile foot-plus, wriggled and leaked over the hippo's lower belly. "You're fine, hon. Go ahead and wreck me."

"Looks nice in there," Jake remarked. "See that thing stretch. Beautiful. Go ahead, Levi, bump your knot up there." The poodle knew what the bloodhound meant, and edged forward. Silence descended over the group except for the sounds of straining and sighing, followed by a single slow clap.

"Bravo," said Cliff. "About as hard as throwing a Vienna sausage into the Grand Canyon."

Analogy aside, it felt damn good and he wasn't even thrusting yet. Maybe it was Aidan's adorable face scrunched up in ecstasy, or the mere fact he was fucking something with more legs than he. Whatever the cause, he wouldn't have any trouble finishing, especially with the other two guys helping out.

"I know it's a while before the sun comes up," Cliff remarked, "but I really need to breed somethin'. Can we get on with it?"

"Be my guest," said Levi, still surprised at his own confident tone. He stiffened his spread legs for a better angle while the hawk kneeled above Aidan's head.

Jake came back into view, shrugging his overalls onto his shoulders. "Man, that's a pretty sight. Too bad I'm kind of a one-and-done guy. You want me to film any of this for, you know, posterity? I bet it'd be pretty popular with the people into fuzzy folk."

"Well…" Levi began, grabbing pawfuls of slick hippo skin to steady himself.

"Let the lad have his first time," Cliff said. "Plenty of full moons for the phone porn." With that, the hawk dragged his fingertips down each side of the hippo's head, ending with some ear rubs.

After a relatively rough start, Levi found a rhythm and started shifting his weight in time with Cliff's thrusts. Not long after that, the poodle bottomed out in Aidan. One more and the hawk bottomed out as well. They had achieved peak penetration.

Cliff offered words of encouragement, though they became fewer and farther between as the hawk eventually lost focus to instinct. Gone was the Bing Crosby voice, replaced by increasingly desperate grunts and the occasional soft creel. Aidan had his head parallel to the ground with Cliff basically fucking his face.

With the hawk setting the pace, Levi found he didn't really have to move much to achieve a nice pleasant throb from the hippo's rump. Whereas before he couldn't have imagined the appeal of getting fucked, watching Aiden made him understand that. Also, some people just needed breeding. He couldn't put it into words, nor did he need to. The hippo's wriggling body told the story.

Jake sat on the nearby log and rifled through his phone, having either lost interest or wanting to leave the threesome in peace.

Aiden spit out Cliff's member, his face suddenly slackened. "Oh fuck, I'm coming." He cast almost-fearful eyes at Levi. "Squeeze me! Please!"

"What, already?" the poodle asked but cut off when he realized how close Aidan really was. It took a second to realize the hippo meant his cock, so the poodle closed his fist below the flared head, almost jerking it away again when he felt—more than saw—the flow through his paw pads. Several thick gobs shot out, landing loudly on Aidan's belly, neck, and moaning mouth. The hardness danced in Levi's grip, as fascinating as it was weird, but the clenching heat of the hippo's tail proved too much. He'd been holding off anyway, so it was only a matter of relaxing certain muscles. His cock jerked to life, throbbing while swelling even larger at the base like a blood-pressure cuff. Then all that tension washed away in a blissful flood of semen.

A lot of semen. Again.

After about ten seconds, when the pleasure had mostly faded but he was still shooting, his question about just how canine he was had an answer. By that time as well, Cliff had passed the point of no return and held himself down, making a nice white puddle on the hippo's neck.

Levi could only dangle his tongue in the air, eyes rolled up to whites, as Aidan's voice somehow made it over the hedonistic chorus lighting his senses afire: "Uh-oh, I know that look when I see it..."

"He'll be back," Jake finished for the hippo.

***

Levi held the drumstick gingerly between his claws and nipped daintily at the meat. Learning to eat with a muzzle had about as shallow a learning curve as walking with a tail, but the poodle didn't want to appear as famished as he actually was. After having his fill of hawk cock, Levi used Jake's towel to clean up while Cliff dressed. Now the three bipeds sat around the remains of the campfire, sharing a big bucket of fried chicken while Aidan munched down on a big bowl of tofu, beans and grasses. As he took particular internal pleasure at separating flesh from bone, the trail mix he'd stashed in the trunk of his car seemed as appetizing as rice cakes to a dieter.

"Thanks for thinking of this," he said, making sure to droop his ears a little to show appreciation. Slowly he was becoming aware of his ability to consciously control body responses that had seemed involuntary. It'd be months before he could match the others in agility, and he harbored a newfound respect for Aidan and his extra legs.

"Oh, this is just part of the shopping list. Nobody gets to go hungry on my watch," Cliff assured the poodle. "Most people can't afford steak every month like that so you get your pork, your high-protein shakes, your tofurkey." The hawk glanced toward the hippo.

Jake swallowed loudly. "Yeah, if you wanna hear somethin' gayer than Aidan, ask him what he calls it."

"I'm not ashamed of my geekdom, so that doesn't work on me. If you must know," Cliff said to Levi, "It began as a joke. A riff on an old song. 'The King Harvest,' I call it." He finished with a feathery flourish, clearly proud instead of shameless.

"And the rest of it?" prodded the hippo.

"You know, because we're 'dancing in the moonlight'?'"

Jake snorted. "Oh, is *that* what we were doin' a few hours ago? Just dancing? I guess that's what the kids're calling it these days."

"I dunno, I kind of like it." All three looked at him with three different expressions. "It's quirky." The poodle shrugged, not having anything else to say.

"That it is," said Jake. "You're gonna fit right in, for better or worse. If you decide to come back."

Cliff patted the nude poodle's ample rear. "Kid's a damn good dancer, we found out." He winked. "I'd be disappointed if you decided not to grace us with your presence again."

The itch began again, and Levi looked to the lightening sky. The light-blue horizon was starting to come up pink. His new friends, despite their smiles and humor, also seemed on edge in their own ways. Clearly the time had come to go their separate ways. Part of him wanted to know what the human versions of them looked like, but he got the feeling that just didn't happen.

"I'll be here. Next month," he said, further heartened when they pulled him into something passing for a hug. No tears, merely good vibes until the next time.

"Sure you don't wanna come back tomorrow?" asked the hippo. "Or are you a one-day-and-done guy?"

"Kind of," Levi replied with a half-shrug. "The other two days I can still use a toilet, so…" The group had a laugh before he trudged off through the undergrowth.

An urgency overtook him, the need to run in the time he had left. The hunting instinct, driven by the power of the moon, feeding a hunger no food could satisfy. He ran through the forest, the fresh damp air filling his lungs, until a minute later he collapsed—heaving—against a tree. All that fresh damp air made his lungs hurt, so he rode out the rest of the change on his back in the nascent morning.

Levi decided instinct could wait until he joined a gym.

Nothing Feathered, Nothing Gained

Resolute

Drasik took the letter from the messenger, broke the seal, and read the death of a four-year trading partnership. Questions filled his head while a buzz of frustration built in his chest, but he pushed both under the surface. "Thank you for bringing this to me," he said, with measured speech and level tone. "Can you carry a reply?"

The small human shook her head. "Sorry, um. Sir? I'm sorry, but I'm just supposed to confirm delivery." To her credit, she didn't stare at him for too long. "I'm bound on other errands. He means no disrespect, I'm sure."

He nodded, and folded the letter into one of his pockets. "I'm sure, young one. And I understand. You may go." The girl bowed her head before jogging back down the street.

Drasik kept his bearing neutral, with tail relaxed and shoulders straight, as he headed to his office and residence. The steady stream of traffic in the lakeward business district of Silvermere kept him from standing out. Most of the passers-by on these streets were used to seeing gryphons and lizardfolk—a term he was growing to dislike, as he certainly wasn't a lizard, but correcting humans could be more trouble than reward. His muzzle-like snout and crest of short horns still drew some glances, while his striated hide and long tail had the occasional head turning to gawk.

Fortunately, they all passed without incident.

A group of four clay brick houses surrounded a fifth building that served as store room and kitchen. Drasik's bordered one of the main city streets, which was perfect for business and tolerable for living. It was home, or close enough to it. A familiar scent touched his nose as he entered through the front door.

"Drasik?" Sianna had been reclining on a row of narrow cushions next to his assistant, but rose with a fluid motion once he was in sight. "Kosk said you might stop back here for lunch, but I didn't want to impose." She inclined her head, tan-feathered crest lifting a fingers-length and tufted ears swiveling his way. Gryphons had odd faces, with a too-inflexible beak and feathers rising and falling in odd patterns, but he'd learned to read her usual range of emotions. Relaxed, yet attentive, if not a little eager to see him.

"Good afternoon," he said, matching her bow with a smile. Kosk stood, but otherwise awaited his call. "You're never an imposition, my friend. All is well, I hope? Can you stay for lunch?"

"It is, and I can." A shaded feather was loose on her chest, drawing his eye, but the rest of her plumage and gray coat of fur were well-groomed. "Though I do have letters for you first."

"Just one moment." He gestured to Kosk and gave a quick series of instructions when he approached. The moss-green male nodded, then set out to find both food and courier. Drasik thought the youth's intellect wasted in years of menial service to elevate his status and assist with negotiations instead of errands, but that was the way of things.

With that done, he pushed into the sitting room and held the door for Sianna. "Come in." His smile returned as she padded past him with the balanced poise of a natural huntress. It was worth admiring for a moment, but rude to stare. He closed the door behind

84

them. "Special deliveries?"

"Just letters," she said after taking a seat on a floor cushion. A moment of searching followed until she brought three sealed envelopes from her leather satchel and held them out, with a practiced grip masking her talons' mediocre dexterity. "None urgent."

He nodded and reached out to take them, fingers brushing talons. Unlike the earlier missive, all three were routine communications. He set them aside, tail swaying as he thought. The Matriarch had entered the city three days ago. Even when she took time to settle in, he'd always received a prompt invitation to attend her and report his work—usually on short notice.

This time, he'd gotten nothing more than word of her arrival.

Sianna, waiting patiently across from him, tilted her head. "Not what you expected?"

He stilled his tail, and briefly explained his thoughts. "I could understand if she had meetings of her own with the merchants," he continued, "but my role is to represent her authority. A direct meeting without my involvement wouldn't be proper. I can't imagine why she would delay, unless she was displeased."

"You still have your own authority, Drasik. The merchants and dock masters trust you, and while she may deliver the goods, you are the one who sits at their tables. Why worry about the Matriarch's displeasure?"

He smiled at her optimism, but she didn't know about the letter. He pulled it from his pocket. "Because a fifth of our business is indefinitely suspended as of this afternoon."

Her ears flattened as she drew back. "What?" She focused on the page and read, pupils narrowed amid green-gold irises. "So that's why you're tense. You got that letter before you arrived?" At his nod, she huffed. "You've told me about that merchant. If he doesn't come around, you might be better off."

"His businesses handle one of every twelve coins flowing through Silvermere's docks. Even if we could sell the goods he'd have bought, we'd do so at a loss."

She smoothed her feathers, shrugged her wings, and her beak parted in her own smile. "I understand. But, what would you tell me to do, if I were worrying three problems ahead of the present?"

"To focus on what you can fix in the here and now," he said, and chuckled. "Or that I should scratch your ears until the stress is gone."

"Good advice. Proper care of gryphons is very important." Her expression wasn't the easiest to read, but her eyes twinkled with mischief. "After the meal, perhaps?"

"Perhaps." He shook his head, rueful. "For now, please, tell me about your work so far."

Her work was, blessedly, routine and uneventful. By the time an apprentice of the house block's chef brought in a large plate of grilled lake fish, fresh fruit, and warm bread, they had moved on to stories of home. Sianna was the lucky one, with an easy day's flight between Silvermere and her clan's home in the Shattered Hills.

His mind wandered further ashore, to home beyond the towering peaks the humans called the Worldspine. Traveling to or from Silvermere took up to two weeks over water. He'd used to travel home more often, before he'd grown accustomed to the human city and at least some of its inhabitants.

Sianna tipped her head back, swallowing a last piece of meat, then dragged her cushion next to his seat. By the time she'd settled, he'd cleaned his fingers and leaned a little to the side—all the better to run his short, trimmed claws through her crest. It didn't take long before she started purring. She didn't have the soft thrum of the small felines that owned humans more than the other way around, but a deep, throaty rumble that might well set the dishes to rattling if encouraged. He laid on plenty of encouragement. She was perhaps the oddest friend he'd made, but she was witty and beautiful and comfortable.

Besides, she wasn't part of the complicated dance of status that often consumed his people. There was a range of statuses for outsiders, if he bothered with propriety, but not having to weigh the sum of her station and standing was a strange relief. Perhaps it was selfish of him to consider that part of their friendship. Then again, she had implied he was something similar to her: not part of her normal world, but welcome in her company in spite *and* because of it.

Sianna pressed her larger head into his palm and glanced up at his face. "Is the stress gone yet?"

He redoubled the scratching and shrugged, not fighting the slight tug of a smile. "I think we're doing this backwards if I'm the one who needs relief."

"I'm sure it works both ways. But, to be serious, would you like the same?"

"It is nice to think about," he admitted, "but I don't have ears or feathers. Preening me is rather impossible."

She considered that, then her warm beak nudged his arm. "Sit beside me. I will make my best effort."

Drasik didn't frown or hesitate, but his mind still worked on her intent as he pulled the chair's cushion onto the floor next to hers. Controlled reactions and social calculations were hazards of his job. She half-crawled closer until her shoulder touched his back. It took some adjustment before his tail and her paws weren't in danger of entanglement, but she coaxed him to recline against her plumage. It really was nice, he reflected. The thick feathers seemed to trap her body heat, and her breath tickled over his hide. The smooth beak trailed from shoulder to neck, then up the back of his head.

"Just relax," she murmured, navigating the crest of short horns along the back of his skull. "The stress does you no good."

He'd have nodded if she wasn't so close. "This is quite nice, thank you." His idle hands felt awkward, and he wanted to turn, to recip-rocate the affections. He thought of something to distract them. "If I may ask, this sort of preening is a bonding activity between gry-phons, correct?"

The beak hesitated in its explorations before poking him. "Drasik, you know you may always ask! And yes, it is a common thing for close friends. Or mates." She paused a moment. "We are, perhaps, not quite close enough for that."

He chuckled, and reached up to rub her neck. "Probably not. But, we are friends, and at least fairly close?"

"Without doubt." She did shift to let him better reach, and he moved closer—the better for their mutual grooming, surely. Her scent wasn't quite earth, wood, or musk but something reminiscent of all three. Proximity only made it stronger. "And for your culture? Do tell me if this is rude or intrusive."

"It isn't," he said, thinking. "But, there's not an easy parallel. Bathing, maybe? It depends on one's status relative to—well, you know." Their people's hierarchies weren't a thing one easily explained to outsiders, but he'd taught her the basics. It was almost odd how much they'd shared, but even though his day-to-day dealings were with humans, he felt richer for their own experiences.

They were still too apologetic, of course, but he took that as a good sign. Neither wanted to hurt the other by ignorance or carelessness.

"It can be anywhere from a professional service to an intimate encounter," he continued, "so I'd say this, here, is something done for a close friendship."

She hummed, and leaned her head against his shoulder. "I'm glad. It'd be quite awkward if I found I was crossing boundaries."

"Momentarily awkward, at worst. I mean, touching one's horns could be considered intimate." He could sense her ears flattening, and he patted her neck before she could think to withdraw. "It's fine, Sianna. I don't really mind." It felt nice, and that was the most justification he dared put to it. If she were his own kind, he might have thought they were knowing advances and responded in kind.

It *had* been a while since he'd been home, and opportunities were scarce so far beyond home shores; while he didn't consider humans objectionable, they weren't exactly an appealing option for courtship. The soft skin and lack of tail were just too strange. Gryphons should have seemed odder still, but Sianna was excellent company and had swayed his opinion like the tide.

"Your company is lovely," she murmured, and glanced at the

slotted window. "But. Much as I'd like to stay, I still have other letters to deliver."

"Of course. Our work is never done, it seems," Drasik said, turning but not quite pulling away. The lingering promise of comfort and companionship kept him by her side. "We should meet again. Dinner here, tomorrow, sixth bell after noon?"

Her purr made a brief return, vibrating against his back and shoulder. "Dinner sounds marvelous, and my work will be finished by then. Hopefully your Matriarch will call on you earlier in the day?"

He paused and considered. Dinner seemed the safest option. Matriarch Oniss would expect attendance at her leisure alone—unless, of course, he had an unavoidable engagement that couldn't be canceled on short notice. Saving a shred of favor wasn't worth clearing an entire day of obligations. "I'll manage. Sixth bell, barring catastrophe upon the city itself."

"I look forward to it," she said, and hummed in appreciation of his touches. "For now, my friend, remember to breathe. The winds will carry you as they will, but you aren't powerless in their grasp."

"'Waves and currents may push and pull, but you still have the strength to swim.' A universal metaphor, I suppose."

"Just so." She glanced down at his tail, which had taken to erratic twitches to match his thoughts. "I can tell it weighs on you."

He did take a breath, at that. Usually he stilled anxious impulses, but he'd let his control slip. "It does, but you are right. I will find a way." It felt wrong, dishonest, to keep wearing the masks his position demanded while around her. He smiled instead. "Part of me wishes I could have you deliver these."

She shifted, and an edge of regret cut through the tranquility. It had been the wrong thing to say, even if true. She worked for convenience rather than necessity. Employment would place her in far more concrete station relative to him—one too far below his position to allow them such things as sitting on the floor and pretending to groom each other.

"I'm sorry," he said, "I just mean—I don't want to imply you ought to work for me." It was heartening to see her ears perked instead of flattened, and crest still relaxed instead of flaring with offense. Cautious curiosity, if he had to name her expression, and he continued, "I mean to say, I trust you, and trust in our friendship." It seemed an incomplete sentiment, and he reconsidered speaking before thinking. Too many missteps could lead to a storm of trouble.

Despite the awkwardness, or perhaps because his tail was plainly twitching again, she nuzzled his shoulder. "I think I understand. It wouldn't work for continuing like this in practice, but if nothing else, at least we'd see each other more?"

That thought settled into place and stuck, apparently the missing piece to his incomplete musings. "Exactly." He almost slumped in relief, but he'd kept just enough poise to avoid dramatic displays. His tail was treacherous enough. "I do want to see you more, Sianna. I value your company."

Her smile banished the rest of his worries. "And I, yours. Even if words fail us at times."

"A heart without words is better than words without heart," he said, smiling back, though the source of the sentiment escaped him. A human proverb, certainly. Their worlds mixed and mingled in the strangest ways.

Sianna made to stand, and Drasik found himself moving with her, as if they'd been on the verge of moving for minutes. Perhaps they had. He pretended not to watch as she snatched a last quick bite of meat, then walked her to the hall and out the main doorway. A large cloud shielded them from the sun, but the air didn't smell like approaching rain; just the city, its people, and Sianna.

"Until tomorrow, my friend," he said, and reached out to brush her neck.

"Until then." She leaned into his palm with a contented hum. With one last smile, she turned and walked down the street. The sway of her haunches and tail caught his eye. The casual motions were less pronounced than his own people's, likely from four legs providing better balance than two. Still, she had quite a nice tail, feathered and furred as it was. He wished he could court a lady with even half that much lithe grace—

He shook his head and wrenched his gaze away, retreating back through the open door.

It had been *far* too long since he'd been home.

***

The evening passed quietly after dispatching his letters. No message arrived. He ate, slept, and woke to a fine morning. No message arrived. Between breakfast and lunch, he took meetings with lesser merchants inquiring after his people's goods, including one from the Aurel Empire—not his favorite human nation, as too much of their legacy grew from the old Kingdom of Ethana. That regime was dead, the trader herself far from unpleasant, and coin was coin.

Still, no message arrived.

As the afternoon drew on, Drasik penned a letter to the Matriarch. He'd already sent customary pleasantries and welcomes when she'd arrived, and asking after a meeting wasn't at all proper. However, he could inform her of changes to the trade contracts and imply a need for her oversight and guidance. So he did, and sent Kosk as the courier—a human was too much of an outsider for such matters.

Kosk was gone for nearly an hour, but he returned with a bark paper card in a sealed envelope. The message, the *invitation,* smelled of sassafras and, vaguely, of home. He held it close to his nose, savoring even the faded reminders. But, the hour grew late, and the sooner he obeyed the nearly immediate summons, the less likely he'd have to bow out for his dinner plans.

Perhaps he should have more consideration for his direct superior, but he found ways to justify the small act of independence.

He arrived as the sun hung between zenith and horizon. The Matriarch had given an address in a less familiar part of the city, and he stopped to admire the painted columns of the rented—or loaned—private house. The single-story building, easily half again as large as his residence, was certainly more upscale than her usual preference. Given the very real threat of a mediocre profit, it bordered on ostentation.

Then again, he suspected the display wasn't for their benefit. Drasik's office was professional, but austere for a merchant lord's tastes. The Matriarch could afford to host high-profile meetings. She had domain over unrestricted trade with the four human nations and employed agents in many ports of call, but Silvermere's neutrality lent it opportunities as robust as they were diverse. Drasik was her familiar, trusted contact. Her first choice for any delicate negotiation. Unless, of course, a last-minute cancellation threatened nearly a quarter of their business.

Then he might be the one blamed.

One way or the other, he had his duty. He steeled himself as he knocked on the door, followed a servant inside, and waited in the main hall until he was recognized and announced.

The secretary, likely the scion of a family of high standing and station, opened the door and stood aside. "Drasik, Master of Contracts and Trades, you are invited before the presence of Sanctioned Matriarch Oniss, First of her Blood, Overseer of the Western Trades." The full list of titles—he had a few, she had at least a minute's worth—wasn't necessary for a private meeting, thankfully. His station had some fair prestige, but only the highest authorities could call on a sanctioned Matriarch.

He cleared his mind, breathing evenly, as he walked into the study turned meeting room. The secretary stepped out, then closed the door.

Books lined wooden shelves set into the walls, chairs stood around a beautiful hardwood desk that smelled far older than it looked, and a mural of Silvermere's history filled the back of the room. The lady behind the desk, back to the door, might have seemed out of place among human trappings if she weren't a force of personality. The room bent to her presence, or so it felt to him.

With wrists crossed before his chest in salute, he awaited her word and will. He was only two stations below her, but her wealth and accomplishment brought her an ocean's worth of standing. Respected as he was, his status below her was clear.

"I admit," the Matriarch said, voice smooth and refined in their native tongue, still not turning, "I was surprised at the content of your message, if not its timing." The letter, he could see, lay on the desk as if left there after a cursory review. "You did well by informing me of this change, Drasik. Could it have been avoided?"

He blinked, but didn't let the question catch him unguarded. "In hindsight, perhaps, Matriarch. Lord Loewe is often unpredictable when he feels it's advantageous. More than that, he's of noble blood, with strong ties to a more traditionalist house of the old Kingdom of Ethana. I suspect non-humans aren't highly regarded in his family."

Mention of the Kingdom made her stiffen, though few would have noticed. Her not-so-distant ancestors had fought Kingdom ships and their armies of conquest. "Then perhaps we're better served without his patronage."

"I thought the same at first," he admitted. "But, this incident aside, he hasn't struck me as spiteful or sectarian." Not unusually so, after some tactful corrections, but those details were a sort of ambassadorial discretion. "He also controls nearly nine percent of the Silvermere Docks market, and buys twice that percentage of our goods, on average."

She finally turned, and her amber eyes narrowed in thought. "So, a fifth of our inventory is at risk because of one contractor's games?"

"Quite possibly, Matriarch."

"Quite possibly," she repeated, commanding an explanation.

"Our other contracts may have room to expand their purchasing power, and his influence is limited beyond his direct holdings. I'm reasonably confident this shipment could be moved before the next arrives, and that we could make up the difference within a year or two if we cannot renegotiate."

She tapped a dyed, blunted claw on the desk. "A year or two we'd planned on growing our profits, and a disruption to our distribution in the meantime." The silky folds and sashes of her dress—not the poofy avalanche of frills some humans wore, but a sleek, elegant design—rippled as she beckoned him closer. "However. I assume you have a plan to 'renegotiate' with this man."

"I do," he said, and laid it out. It was a ploy, he was almost certain, and success meant confronting the bluff without closing the door on what had been a mutually profitable partnership. Then again, the man *was* sometimes unpredictable, and his withdrawal could be from an unshakeable conviction; he didn't trouble her with that explanation, beyond that the most circumspect implication that alternatives be considered, if not prepared.

And while he explained, his mind worked on the oddity of their whole meeting. Cool but cordial pleasantries usually preceded his briefing, and she would share news of home that couriers and even the trading ships' officers often lacked. The contract was a critical concern, but there was a certain decorum, if not ceremony, to official business. Something had changed, and he couldn't tell if it was him, her, or more.

"Good," she said once he'd finished. "I will send instructions on executing your suggestions. Your advice, as always, is keen. Is your report concluded?"

He blinked, but kept his tail still and didn't hesitate. "There are no other urgent matters, Matriarch. But, I—"

"Then our business—," she said, overlapping his words, then stopped. She had the right to keep speaking, and she'd been about to conclude the meeting as quickly as she'd started it. Yet another abnormality to consider. Silently, she gestured for him to continue.

"Begging your forgiveness," he said, "but I'd like to ask after our homeland? It's been too long since I've heard news."

"There is very little news. You haven't heard?"

That brought him pause. For humans, 'little news' meant nothing had happened to disrupt the status quo. For their people, it meant a significant event, something that overshadowed anything else worth reporting. "I've heard rumors only, nothing worth consideration."

She tilted her head. "I had thought word might have reached you already. Rebels launched attacks against our border posts and burned two of our winter granaries in the capital itself. They were quite bold, but their numbers are few. Tides and rains willing, they will be crushed by the end of the year."

It wasn't war, but it was close. There was always dissent, always discontent with the weight of standing on one's status, but such had always been the way of things. If rebels had managed to destroy modestly fortified warehouses in the heart of the capital, they were either far more resourceful or far more numerous than she'd suggested. Would the harvest cover the losses? He didn't know nearly enough.

"Jaxen will provide you a written report tomorrow." That had to be the secretary. "Then our business here is concluded."

He realized his moment had passed, and he crossed his wrists over his chest and lowered his gaze. "My service is yours."

"Yes, it is," she murmured, as if thinking aloud. She took two slow steps closer. "These upheavals remind me that change is inevitable, and that loyalty deserves reward." It wasn't a question, and he didn't respond. "Do stand easy, Drasik. I have a proposition for you."

He let his arms drop to his sides and took in a breath. It was bound to be interesting. "I'm curious to hear it."

The hint of a smile, not lacking in warmth even with its hidden edges, played over her face. "You are dedicated, skilled. Quite handsome. I would offer you a place as my... adviser, in all matters of trade. An opportunity to elevate yourself, and then you could command the merchant fleet. No more sitting in human cities waiting for trade to come to you. No more chasing after contracts. You are talented, and I wouldn't see your experience wasted."

His heart had jumped at the mention of elevation, and it took all his poise to keep his tail from an excited sway. "That is a very generous offer," he said, keeping a grip on his nerves lest he forget it was a negotiation. "And you are most kind in your praise." It wouldn't be polite to ask for the catch—and there would be a catch.

Her smile grew in both size and calculation as she took another slow step forward. "There's another reason I want you closer, Drasik. My subordinates are too low in station to serve all my needs, and social connections back home are, shall we say, *complicated*." She was near enough to easily touch, if either of them wanted to, and she looked right into his eyes. "But you, yes. Your company would be a joy. If you come with me, I would ask of you: be my consort, in pleasure as well as business."

Given the events of the past days, it didn't surprise Drasik nearly as much as it should have. He still blinked, still took in a breath, and still let his mind race through the many consequences and complications. She had the clout to make good on her offer of elevation. If she also placed him in charge of the fleet, he could earn assurance of his new status in a few short years. Home would be a regular sight, not an increasingly distant memory.

One question arrested his hopes: how much freedom would he have to give up? Being consort wouldn't let her force intimacy, of course, but he would serve at her pleasure and for her pleasure. It would behoove him to stay available to her desires.

Unfortunately, he couldn't keep from imagining the consorting. His eyes moved before he could stop them, a treacherous slip of his poise. She had a supple build, softer than one used to physical exertion but still strong and agile in her own right. Unlike humans, her chest was as flat as his, which meant he could let his gaze drift.

He didn't dare look any further down, towards the now animated tail curling just enough to the side to see, but not far or fast enough to seem like an overt invitation. He wanted to stare, and maybe even do more than stare.

The promise of pleasure was all too tempting.

"You never rush into decisions, I've noticed," she said, studying him. "I've always admired that. Restraint, due consideration, but you make the right choice in good time."

"I gather all the information I can." He hoped to use his 'due consideration' to stall while he kept thinking. Something still didn't add up. "Then I act. Just as you do, if I may say, Matriarch."

"Just as I do," she echoed, taking one last step and reaching up to run fingers over the shoulder of his tailored coat. Every breath let him scent her mix of perfumes, from the familiar aromatic bark to the nectarine hint of royal flowers; each element was faint, subtle, but they complemented each other well enough to become *her* scent, one he couldn't quite isolate or dismiss as artificial.

He exhaled, trying to keep the haze from settling on his thoughts and robbing him of his poise, if not wit. He felt himself stirring, readily responding to her presence and suggestion after barely a touch. It didn't help that despite his reservations, his instincts said her interest was serious, if not genuine.

Both hands were now on him, and her lips came close to his ear. "We can retire to my private chamber. You don't have to decide now, or tonight. But, I can show you the benefits of your new station." She sighed, then took half a step back as if reconsidering. "If this is discomforting, forgive me. I… well, my status precludes most companionship, and there are none that I trust to keep so close, even for a night." She seemed ready to say more, but closed her mouth before she could.

"I, ah. I'm not uncomfortable, at least how you fear." His pulse drummed in his chest and palpably, almost conspicuously, throbbed between his legs. Thoughts felt sluggish and trivial. His hands twitched, and he realized he'd nearly been ready to embrace her in return, if she hadn't withdrawn. "But it is a very, a significant change. It's a lot to consider."

She nodded, though the explanation sounded simplistic to his ears. Perhaps the same rush of feeling clouded her mind as well, unless she was just humoring him. "My invitation is still open, of course. Pleasure shared is pleasure earned."

He tried not to consider it, and still considered it far too readily.

The thought of Sianna, waiting in vain for a friend who wouldn't arrive, snapped him from his reverie. If he left soon, he could easily make it back in time for dinner. If he gave in, it could easily take until sunset to get properly acquainted, assuming their desires didn't keep them going well into the night.

"I'm afraid I must decline, as I have a prior engagement." It seemed inconsiderate, but he'd practiced his poise for too long to let it slide under pressure—even if enjoyable pressure. He chose his next words without breaking stride. "Your offer tempted me to send my regrets and forget it, but it wasn't the only obstacle. The truth is, this broken contract and now news of strife weighs on my mind. I fear I'd be a lackluster companion this night, and even if I weren't under your service, you'd deserve nothing short of my best performance."

"I see." A shade had fallen on her expression at the start, but it washed away once he'd continued. Her hands left his clothing to smooth down hers, and then she curtly nodded, professionalism returned. "Yes, I imagine you've had quite the day." The stern set of her eyes also faded as she studied him, and she let out a soft breath. "And I value your integrity. It's no surprise you're just as dedicated and forthcoming in your personal affairs."

"My service is yours." He kept his expression neutral, and made his play. "With your leave, I would like to think through the opportunity."

Her eyes drifted downwards before flicking back up to meet his. "Yes, you may depart. Report on the recovery of the canceled contract. I will send what we know of the rebels. Unless, of course, you'd prefer to exchange the news personally. I will be in the city for a short while longer." Her smile returned, though an undercurrent tinged the invitation. The offer wouldn't last.

It was just one more thing to think about as he left the office and started down the street back home.

***

"Just draft a standard reply to these two messages, and prepare this for a courier tomorrow." Drasik handed the card, a request for a meeting with the recalcitrant Loewe, to Kosk. "Then you are released from your duties for the evening."

The young assistant blinked a couple times, but didn't twitch or exclaim. He'd been practicing his poise. Good. "I understand. I can remain close if you need to summon me—"

Drasik held up a hand, forestalling the rest of the offer. "I will handle anything that arises. You've earned the right to enjoy yourself." Besides, he needed some time alone, with the exception of the impending dinner.

"My service is yours," he said, saluting, and then busied himself with pen and paper. He'd already sent payment for the dinner to the residence block's chef, with extra for delivery. By the time the food arrived he'd likely seek out the fleet's sailors to drink and socialize. He'd taken news of the rebellion well enough, though without details it was hard to do more than adjust to the reality.

Beyond that, there was little to talk about. It was the new way of things.

Drasik had just seen him off when a *whoosh* of air rattled the windows; a gryphon, probably Sianna, had just passed low over the house. The roof had a balcony theoretically large enough to land on, but she preferred room to run off the momentum of a landing instead of coming to a hard stop. Flight was both marvel and mystery, so he'd made the offer out of politeness and didn't complain that she chose the clearing down the street instead. It also meant waiting for her to walk down the block, which had him pacing along the front of the hall, tail flicking nearly enough to thump against the walls.

Then, the knock came, and he tried to compose himself before opening the door.

"Thank you," she said, brushing past his thigh as he gestured her towards the sitting room. There was a more formal dining table, but the chairs were too small to comfortably support her, so they arranged themselves on floor cushions next to the coffee table and couch. The former would serve them well enough. Then she dragged her cushion closer and nosed him, ears perked. "Are you well?"

He nodded, perhaps too quickly, and reached up to brush her feathered neck. "I'm well enough. Please, tell me about your day."

"Uneventful." The word came out slowly, tone skeptical, and her head turned to better look at him with one eye. "You met with your Matriarch, didn't you? What happened?"

He debated telling her it was also uneventful, or that he was just worried over the asinine contract, but he couldn't hide the truth. It wasn't just because that eye was too keen, or because she knew him too well, but because he did need to tell her. The offer, traveling with the Matriarch, meant leaving Silvermere—and her. So he told Sianna about the war, his suspicions, and even the offer.

She drew back at the last one, crest rising. "I'm curious. She— oh, how do you say it. Tried to... persuade you with sex?"

"Seduce me?"

"Yes." She knew the two common human tongues well, and had picked up a surprising amount of his own, but he doubted she'd heard *that* sort of language in any polite company. "Isn't that improper since she's higher in station?"

He shrugged, and smoothed down the ruffled feathers. "She was offering a position where that wouldn't matter." With a soft sigh, he forced himself to confront one of his misgivings. "But, it isn't normal. She must think I'd be a very good consort to offer it. Unless," he said, then trailed off.

"Unless?" She turned to regard him, beak opening to ask more, but she stopped and let the question hang until he'd thought through the answer.

"Unless there's something else she wants, given everything that's changing." He still needed to know the full context of the home situation, but at least he knew the Matriarch well enough to read her. "I mean, she *was* interested in me, but she's not one to be impulsive, or only consider one angle. Maybe she needs me for something." And she had implied she couldn't trust anyone back home, given how many status-seekers would only see her wealth and prestige.

"That could very well be," Sianna said, tilting her head to consider. "I wish I were better versed in your politics. I'm of little help in this mystery."

He snorted and leaned closer, all the better to stroke his palm down her back, right between those huge, magnificent wings. "Honestly, sometimes you're even more a help to me than Kosk. I couldn't talk about any of this to him. He's too far below me."

"It wouldn't be proper," she said, nodding her understanding.

"Exactly."

A twinkle formed in her eye as she fixed it on him. "Less improper than sitting on the floor, petting a gryphon?"

"And here I thought petting a gryphon was always proper." He gave up pretense and kneeled right next to her, putting both hands into grooming and caressing her downy coat. A few stray feathers fell away as he brushed with his trimmed claws. "Sitting on the floor is just a matter of convenience."

She hummed, or perhaps it was a low purr. "I can't argue the point."

The food would arrive at any moment, but he didn't feel like filling the time with idle small talk. It was relaxing, if not freeing, to just enjoy the close company after all the revelations and machinations. The side of her beak brushed his muzzle as she tried to resume her mock-preening, though neither of them worried enough to apologize. He wondered if she had similar reasons for seeking the close contact, or if the more sociable gryphons took it for granted.

It was a question for later.

"I'm glad you decided to come here instead of, well." She trailed off, probably unsure if she was about to offend.

Fortunately, he was in agreement. "I am too. I have to admit, her offer was tempting," he murmured, taking in her warm, familiar scent. "Especially since it's, uh." The tip of his tail nearly set to squirming, but he controlled himself.

There was a space, a hesitation, before Sianna tentatively continued the thought. "Been a while?"

"A while, yes." Honesty. It was a novel thing, being so honest and open. "Maybe too long."

"I can relate. Though at least your hands are flexible?" She ruffled her wings and resettled them against her sides. "Sometimes I feel the only real release comes from a proper mounting."

That idea *did* have him squirming, just a little, but he waved away her noise of concern. It was just talk. "Hands are no substitute for the real thing. I can only imagine the struggles you have." He tried to keep his imagination in check, but they were quite thoroughly on topic.

She made another little hum before mantling a wing around his back. "They're not so difficult. Just inconvenient. The companionship makes it all the better in the end."

"So, something like this?" He realized the implication a heartbeat later. "With another gryphon, of course."

"Of course," she echoed, chuckling. "Though if I may admit something?"

"Go ahead."

She touched her beak to his horns, ears flattening. "I think it's a shame we're not the same species."

He teased at one of the tufted triangles. "Oh? For better preening?"

"Yes. Yes, for that."

"Or," he continued, heart beating as he dared add, "for what happens after the preening?"

She actually shivered, and the wing tightened against his back. Odder still, he felt himself stirring at his own implication. "That," she said, "is the sort of tease that would lead to such things."

"Duly noted." He leaned against her shoulder, though between the wing's comfort and the banter he'd started to feel warm. Moving away didn't seem like an option. "Is it strange to say I feel the same?

You'd be quite beautiful no matter what form you took."

Another chuckle, and then she licked the base of a shorter horn near his ear. "Flattery, too? I see why your Matriarch tries courting you."

"She hasn't seen this side of me," he said, not quite caring what that implied when being close to her felt exhilarating. And did she know what that gesture meant? He'd explained it, he thought, but maybe she hadn't realized.

"Don't stop on my account." Her tongue was short, strong, and surprisingly warm on his hide. She knew, or at least suspected.

"I don't want to. Nor should you." Now it was his turn to shiver as he tilted his head in invitation, and she obligingly worked down to his neck.

A faint, pleased growl came as her reply, and she shivered again as he worked claws between her wings and over her chest. Heated breath tickled over his neck, faster than usual, and he realized he was starting to pant as well. She was so very different, but she was warm, and close, and he couldn't think of a reason to keep from getting closer.

His muzzle brushed her beak, and then their tongues, independently exploring, met for a brief moment. They didn't quite withdraw, but there was a sense of change, of a boundary about to be crossed. There was a knock at the back door, but he didn't care about anything other than the two of them.

"Do you want to keep going?" he asked.

"Yes." She shivered again, and her ears had flared right at him, along with her crest. "But, what if we're not able to? We should—" Then she stopped, ears perking towards the hall.

He wanted to say it didn't matter, to ask her what she wanted, to throw all caution and decorum to the waves and winds, but he realized there'd been a second knock. A moment later, a key rattled and clicked the latch open.

They moved apart, sharing a wide-eyed look. After the frozen heartbeat of panic came and went, Drasik made a quick sweep of his fingers to smooth down her feathers, then made sure his tunic wasn't too disheveled as he stood. "They'll only be here a few seconds," he said, "then we can, uh, find out." He tried not to think about what had been happening, and about to happen. They weren't lovers treading familiar shallows, and the heat of the moment was already fading to an awkward silence.

He turned to face the inner door, just past Sianna and the table. Poise. He breathed to collect himself, standing straight, allowing confidence to mask any shock or guilt—acting flustered was a sure way to raise suspicion, even if they were no longer in a compromising position.

Her gaze leveled at his crotch, and she smoothly moved her head between the rather noticeable tent in his pants and the view of the human bringing a tray into the room. *That* was definitely compromising. Not missing a beat, he placed a hand between her ears in silent thanks, and perhaps to steady himself.

Poise wouldn't cover everything, it seemed.

"Your food delivery, sir? And for your, um, guest." The male moved towards the table, but didn't set the tray down until Drasik gestured with his free hand. "Seared meat in sauce, steamed and spiced vegetables, and mixed grains. All ingredients are guaranteed safe for nonhuman consumption, as requested." Red tinged his face, as he likely realized the way 'nonhuman' had sounded.

He decided to let it pass. "Thank you, that will be all. If you'd please lock the door again on your way out?"

"Of course, honored guests." Not quite appropriate, but better. He bowed, and withdrew, shutting both doors and locking the last from the outside.

Drasik relaxed, smelling the food as he took a breath. It really did smell delicious, but he regretted the interruption. He looked down at Sianna, unsure what to say, but she'd cocked her head to examine the shape still straining at the tailored pants. Evidently, there was more pent up lust than he'd anticipated. Despite the brief scare, despite the control and calm granted by his poise, the arousal wasn't fading—and her stare, equal parts curious and hungry, actually fueled the still-growing tension.

Then, she turned, and touched the smooth, curved front of her beak to his loins, feeling the stiffness through the fabric. His breath departed in a soft rush, and his fingers wove into her feathered crest.

"Not satisfied with the meat on the table?" His heart beat faster for better reasons than surprise.

"It smells good," she murmured, breath even warmer than her beak. Whether she meant the food or *him* wasn't clear; her sense of smell was poor in comparison, but far from useless. "But, I'm not terribly hungry this moment. Are you?"

He caressed her, and shook his head. "Not yet." The interruption had cleared his mind enough to think through what they'd been about to do—and the option was still on the table, so to speak. Contingencies and consequences flitted through his mind, and then washed away like a receding tide. He knew Sianna, trusted her, and enjoyed her company. There was no need to dance around social strata or worry about schemes. His only two worries were how to pleasurably fit their quite different bodies together, and how to handle their relationship after that.

The former, naturally, demanded his full attention.

"Not yet," he repeated, voice breathy as she nuzzled him again. "But, we can work up an appetite? If you're fine with going that far."

She tilted her head to give him a flat stare with one eye. The beak still pressed to his arousal was a clear answer, but her features softened as she realized the question behind it. "I am, if you are. Pleasure shared between friends is common enough for my kind. What of yours?"

"Complicated. For us? Doesn't matter." He curled his fingers under her beak to lift her head, and bent to meet her halfway. She shivered as he pressed his muzzle to her ear, and warmly murmured, "I want you."

"Skies above, Drasik, you'd better remove that clothing before I tear it off."

He grinned, and kissed the side of her beak. "Here, or my bed-room is just past—"

"Bedroom," she growled, cutting him off. Her tongue brushed his lips, and then she started towards the door, rubbing the length of her body against him as she passed. The long, sinuous, and furred feline tail curled around his neck before drawing the tip under his chin, though she kept the fan of feathers at its base low enough that he couldn't make out what was underneath. She glanced over her shoulder, eyes alight, and he stood to follow.

The single door down the hall was narrow enough that Sianna had to tuck her wings in. He helped her through, mostly with a firm squeeze to her rump, which had her purring. He closed the door behind them, turned up the pair of lamps, and started unbuttoning his vest. She barely glanced around before her keen stare followed the motions of his hands.

"Might take some experimenting," he said as he tossed the gar-ment and undershirt aside. His chest and belly had soft, pale green hide, which she likely hadn't seen in full before. After kicking off the indoor sandals, he leaned on the bed and bent to undo the cuffs on his ankles. Formal clothing could get quite tedious, he noted, when one had a gryphoness to entertain. "I don't know if I can mount you, or if the bed would work better?" His mind tried to work on the problem, and it threatened the mood.

She was on him before he could stand. A deep, almost predatory growl rumbled in her chest, and that tongue bathed his chest, his neck, and then his muzzle. "You worry too much, handsome male." One of her talons braced her weight on the bed. The other groped his thigh, though she was mindful of the claws. "Take these off. We'll go from there."

He reached back, unclasping the over-tail fastenings, pulled the waist of both it and his underbreeches over his lingering arousal, then pushed and kicked until he was quite thoroughly naked before her—which, he granted, was her usual state. The air was cool, but the warmth radiating from her feathered, furred body more than made up the difference, even as she drew back to examine him.

"So this is what you look like," she murmured, as if to herself, and bent down to directly nuzzle his half-hard length. It jumped at her touch, and within moments it stood proud, the thicker base ever so slightly spreading the slit that usually kept his malehood safe. "Mating will be no trouble, I think. Different from a gryphon, thicker at the head. And are these…?"

He took in a short, shallow breath as she flicked her tongue over his ridges. "Gryphons don't have those?"

She shook her head, and gave him another lick before prowling forward and rubbing her beak alongside his muzzle. He mirrored her motions after a moment, slightly confused but following her lead. Perhaps it was the gryphon version of a kiss or embrace. When she withdrew enough, he tilted his head to press his lips to the front of the beak, and felt her hesitate before relaxing and letting him guide the kiss. He added a little tongue, and when she parted her beak to follow suit, it wasn't long before she got into the interplay, the sharing of breath and warmth and intimacy.

"How strange," she murmured, but her purr and ruffled feathers belied thorough enjoyment. "Though, not *too* strange. Unless your kind has unusual mating habits?"

"They're normal to us?" He shrugged, and nearly lost his line of thought as her chest feathers tickled over his softly pulsing length. "I, ah. She spreads her legs, or lifts her tail, and takes my arousal into her nethers, then there's thrusting until our release. I don't think it's any different from—"

"It isn't," she said, cutting him off, partly by pushing him onto the bed until he was all but lying on it. "And I want that, very, very badly." The bed creaked as she climbed atop it, but it didn't seem ready to collapse.

"You and me both." He looked up. Sianna practically loomed over him, like a huntress over her prey, and it drove home the reality that she was half again his size, if not more. That posed a problem. "This, uh. May not work well?"

She tilted her head, and then licked his snout. "Perhaps not." One of her talons rose, letting him roll out beside her. "You should get behind me."

His mouth went dry, pulse thrumming in his chest and loins, and tried not to scramble over the bed linens. Part of him, the part still capable of higher thought, warned that claws and bed linens didn't mix. That part faded to a background buzz as she hiked her feathered and furred tail, revealing thick and shapely haunches. He was a little surprised as he saw what lay between them. There was little modesty when clothing was so inconvenient, but the unavoidable glimpses had only revealed a part in the fur, barely more than a suggestion of her female anatomy.

This time, aroused as she evidently was, he couldn't have missed the flush, inverted teardrop standing out from the surrounding fuzz. A bead of her fluids trailed down the sensitive flesh. The smell was far richer than he'd expected, mixed with a strange, heady sort of musk—likely an instant hook for a male gryphon. He was no gryphon, but he was more than eager to answer her invitation.

There was, of course, another problem.

"Could you, um," he said, lamely placing a hand just above her tail to try and guide her downward. Neither standing nor kneeling would let him line up for mating. She followed his lead, thankfully, and he sucked in a breath as his tip bumped fur, then heated, slick flesh. "Thank you, beautiful."

His other hand spread her folds, exploring, and she pushed back against his palm with a soft croon. He'd just wanted a sense of her, but now that he could tease and please, he found himself working his fingers around her entrance. With care for his claw, he slipped a digit inside her, marveling at the intense warmth of her body and the ripple of muscles around the intrusion. His shaft throbbed in reply, as if jealous.

It wasn't the only protest, it turned out. "In me," Sianna growled over her shoulder, ears flat and gaze just a little clouded with lust. He thought to coax a 'please' out of her, or at least to give her more of a head start in case he didn't last, but the backward push of her hindquarters nearly toppled him off balance, if not the bed. *"Now."*

Never one to argue with a lady in charge, he grunted assent and spread her folds again, guiding himself to her entrance with his other hand. The brief resistance gave way, likely a ring of muscle relaxing. The hand not on his shaft flew to her haunch, holding tight as he sank into her hot, velvety passage, aided by her slick natural fluids.

It was almost unreal to look up and see her large, lithe form, to know he was coupling with a female so very far removed from his species, but she was exotic, enticing, and surprisingly erotic as she arched and flicked her tail to the side. It let him lean forward and brace some of his weight against her back.

His hips pressed flush to her furred rump after a few slow push-es, leaving him comfortably deep in her grip. "Need a moment," he breathed, trying to reconcile the foreign sensations of feathers and fur with the familiar thrill of mating an eager female. He had to adjust if he didn't want to disappoint her with a quick finish.

Fortunately, she voiced wordless agreement, even encourage-ment. He hoped he wasn't too small for her liking. There was only one way to find out. He pulled back, fingers digging into fur as her silky flesh tugged and tightened as if loathe to let him go, then pushed as she relaxed.

"Yes," she said, almost a hiss. She matched his motion as best as her half-kneeling, half-crouching position allowed. "More, Drasik. Harder. I'm not some fragile human."

He felt fire in his belly, already working his hips at a steady tempo, unable to care that they weren't the same. Or maybe he liked the way he could dig his claws into her fur and feel her clench around him in response, how her gasps and groans mingled with his pants and grunts, only adding to the primal carnality of it all.

They didn't have to dance around politics or status as friends. Now they could rut for pleasure's sake and nothing more.

The way she quivered when he pressed his ridges down over her sensitive spots had him grinning and angling his hips for more of the same. The sound of fabric starting to rip gave them both pause.

"Sorry." She lifted a talon, extricating the claws from the small holes in the bedsheet. "I can move?"

"Not worried about it," he said, not wanting to stop. He forced something approaching thought to break through the heated haze of lust and pleasure. A shiver followed, and he couldn't help but grind his hips against her rump before pulling out. The chill of the air on his wet shaft almost drove him forward again. "Actually, here. Can you lie on your side? Like this."

Loathe as she was to stop, she followed his guidance. The bedding wasn't free from the threat of her claws, but he'd scored them enough that they were done for anyway. He licked his lips, helped lift her hind leg, and moved in to straddle the one still on the bed. She caught on and turned her hips. Both leg and tail rose to give him room as he guided himself back in. If anything, she was even hotter than before, and he hugged her leg to his chest.

He could have sworn his first thrust took him deeper than any of the ones before.

"This is different," she murmured, cocking her head to watch him take her.

"That's not the best part." He smirked, keeping one arm wrapped around her leg while dropping his newly freed hand to tease over her folds. "I know I'm probably small, but—"

"Right there!" The interruption was both verbal outburst and hot internal squeeze. "Yes, right there." His words registered a moment later. "You're fine, lover, but *don't stop*."

Lover? It might not be the best term, but it sounded good. "As you wish," he growled, twisting his hips to let her feel those ridges again. If he wasn't too busy pounding her, he'd feel like laughing. He'd needed this: the pleasure, the freedom, and the intimacy. He'd needed *her*, though he'd been too preoccupied to realize it. Wind and tides, but he'd *wanted* her since even before the previous day's 'preening' session.

So, he let go, and took her.

Their mingled scents filled the air with the wet, lewd sounds of their mating. His fingers found the thick nub a few claw-widths above her entrance. A few tweaks and rubs had Sianna writhing and moaning beyond what he'd seen before. The twitches of her thigh against his front might have worried him, as the spasming muscles were capable of launching her into the air and, more than likely, of breaking him in half.

He was too far gone to care. If anything beyond pleasure given and pleasure taken registered, it was surprise that he'd lasted as long as he had.

The surging tension, very near to breaking, had set his breath to ragged panting. His thrusts becoming erratic bucks of his hips, tail lashing behind him. Deep in his core—sensibly hidden and safe, unlike so many other creatures who kept their parts hanging free—his loins churned and prepared their load. Biology and instinct hardly cared that breeding her was impossible.

With one last thrust and a half-choked groan, he felt the heat, the tension, break like a wave upon the rocks.

A rush of pleasure stole his senses, far more intense than he'd felt in months, if not years. He missed home, but Sianna put most of his past lovers to shame. She tensed around him, as if trying to coax his climax along. The attempt to grind against her shuddered to a halt as his muscles locked up. His shaft twitched inside her, pressure welling up until he shot the first load of his seed into her depths.

It was all he could to stay upright. The brush of his fingers, and perhaps the heat of his own release, set her off in turn.

Her hips and leg bucked, nearly throwing him back, and he clung to her as she keened, back arching, every muscle he could feel suddenly alive and twitching. Her inner grip turned from enticing ripple to needy undulation that wouldn't let him pull out even if he tried. He whined, the pleasure spiking nearly to pain as he was nearly spent. He kept his death grip on her leg, teeth gritted as he rode out what felt like a second climax.

Dark spots filled his vision even as he gasped for breath, but even the overstimulation wasn't worth giving up for a heartbeat.

The weight of her leg became too much to support as the pleasure ebbed, and he half-collapsed against her along with it. He wasn't sure which of them was hardest hit by the afterglow. He also wasn't sure how long they leaned on each other, panting, before he made a serious attempt to move. The smell of sex, now enriched by his virile contribution, got even stronger as a wet *pop* preceded a rivulet of mixed fluids on his withdrawal.

If her claws hadn't ruined the sheets, their romp would leave quite a mess. He couldn't bring himself to care when he could just cuddle up against her belly and chest instead, especially when she pulled him closer into the embrace with wing and foreleg.

"That," she said, voice almost more of a hum, "was even better than imagined."

He smiled and stroked through her feathered chest. The softness was far from unfamiliar, but it was a very different thing to nestle against her without anything between them, physical or otherwise. "Agreed. You are amazing."

"As are you." The limbs gently squeezed him, and he hugged her, feeling her powerful heart slow to a relaxed drumbeat. "I should have realized sooner that we could share this."

"You and me both," he said, feeling his softening length brush over her fur. "Mm, but, this was the right time. Or as right as it could get." His thoughts were sluggish, still, and he made a belated connection. "So you imagined this before, hmm?"

She stirred, then chuckled. "Mostly when we were on the floor, and definitely when you stood to greet that human." A sultry purr followed. "I liked my greeting much better."

He moved his hips in a teasing little circle against hers. "I'll bet you did. Thank you for blocking his view, by the way."

"Of course." Consciously or not, she pressed closer in response. "Though it was, perhaps, selfish."

"Wanted to get a good look at me? I might have done the same."

"That," she said, feathers ruffling, "and I didn't want an awkward moment to ruin my chances at getting more than a look."

He grinned, remembering that feeling, and leaned up to kiss her—or try to, as being hip-to-hip meant his head barely reached her neck. Their sizes were hard to compare when they were standing, given the height difference, but sitting, cuddling, and sex all dispelled the illusion that they were similar, and the latter certainly called attention to the difference. He had trouble deciding whether it was more enticing or intimidating—and he suspected that the intimidation factor only excited him further. The thoughts lasted until she bent down to touch beak to lips.

Their kissing, such as it was, still made for an odd alternation between his style with mingled tongues, care taken to avoid the sharp edges inside her beak, and the sort of side-to-side, back-and-forth nuzzling she preferred, with occasional licks and lots of purring on her part.

When their tongues met, they turned their heads and mingled more properly, and parting for breath meant following her lead, such as it was. It was the strangest rhythm he'd ever found with a partner, but his heart still thudded with enthusiasm as they shared breaths, and the awkward fumbles and mumbled apologies grew more infrequent.

He suspected practice would make them quite comfortable with the other's preference and the switches between them. That raised questions on what 'practice' meant for them, but those would wait.

At some point, they'd started moving more than just their heads. His malehood was back at half mast, though slow to respond beyond that, and she didn't seem too intent on escalating beyond idle grinding. Part of him wanted to bury himself in that most wonderful embrace again, but the stamina to rut for hours on end hadn't quite lasted past his second decade of life.

Besides, other needs demanded his attention.

"If you don't mind," he said, reaching up to run tender fingers behind her ears, "I'd like to share a dinner with you, after I clean us off?"

She hummed, an unmistakably satisfied sound, and then those ears flattened as her stomach growled. "Yes, that would be lovely. And thank you in advance for the grooming. Making a mess and ignoring it is fun until it dries in your fur."

He winced. "I can only imagine."

"But," she continued, leaning in to plant a slow lick over his crest, "don't get me *too* clean. Just in case the food works up another appetite."

He laughed and kissed her throat. The willpower to move was slow in coming, more so when his attempt to shimmy out from her embrace mostly led to rubbing himself along the length of her nethers, still slippery, heated, and all too inviting. Surely a little more wouldn't hurt.

"Drasik." Her voice had a low, sultry edge. "If you end up inside me, you'll have to finish what you start."

A reasonable objection didn't surface until her stomach growled again, and with a reluctant sigh he pulled away and extricated himself from their tangle of limbs. After stretching, he gave her a kiss, then went to relieve himself and fetch damp cloths. The washing was surprisingly quick work—though he didn't have to be thorough, yet—and he put on smallclothes as she ducked into the bathing room.

Much of the food was just as delicious cold, thankfully, and they leaned against one another as they ate. This was the part where the questions started, he knew, and his mind had already set to working on them.

Sianna beat him to it. "I hope," she started, ears drooping as she hesitated. His smile seemed to encourage her, and she took a breath. "I don't mean to imply anything, but I hope this doesn't complicate your dealings with the Matriarch."

He snorted and wrapped an arm over her neck. "If she knocked on the door right now and asked, I'd say no."

She nodded, exhaling softly, and mantled her wing over his back. "Is it wrong to say I'm glad?"

"It may be the afterglow talking, but." He forced himself through a brief internal debate. "I don't know. I get the feeling it may be a bad deal."

"Even though she offers you elevation?"

"The chance at it, at least a year down the road. I'd be entirely dependent on her good graces until then." He shook his head. "No. She isn't unkind, but if I get taken in, I doubt I'll find an easy way out. And I'd have to leave you behind." He turned to kiss her beak. "After tonight, I don't want to."

She eyed him fondly, then picked a piece of meat and swallowed it. "So what will you do, if you say no?" Her tone hoped for *when* instead of *if.*

He considered for a few breaths. "Continue as I have. No, no. I need to do more." A plan started to form, and he let it come into focus. "I need to get involved in politics again. I need to find out what's going on at home—if she's offering this, her position might be in danger. Trade with humans isn't exactly popular even when it's profitable. Maybe she's thinking to save me?" He shook his head. "No, it doesn't matter. I need to get more information, send messages to my contacts back home. Maybe even go back home, if it comes to that."

She watched him with a keen yet tender gaze, though her ears dipped at the last part. "I would miss you if you go," she said, "but I understand. If you need me to fly messages, my wings are yours, you know."

He frowned. "I don't think I can pay you now that we've—"

"As a favor, not a job," she said, before he could finish. "You are worth it."

"Thank you." He kissed her. "But. If I go home, you could come with? Gryphons aren't ill-regarded, and you'd be a privileged guest of mine."

"I think I'd like that." She smiled, in her perked ear, opened beak way. "I'll need to learn more about status, if our mating changes that."

That led right into one of the big questions. "Intimacy between friends, no. More than that, though…" There was no simple answer.

She paused, and then nodded. "We will speak more on the subject, I'm sure."

"It'll take a lot of talking, if that's a road we consider." It was his turn to smile. "But, if we do, I know you'd be worth every word."

"You are too kind, my friend." Her beak found his lips, and the moments passed them by.

When they parted, something else came to mind. "Would you object to leaving? I know you have your deliveries, and I don't want you to feel obligated to me."

She chuckled. "The money is for convenience, not necessity. Even if you were to dump me in the middle of the wilderness, I have slept under the stars and hunted for my meals for much of my life. I'd be fine."

"I'd never leave you like that."

"I know," she said, nuzzling him.

"Besides, I'd probably be your first meal if I did."

She frowned. "We don't eat speaking beings, Drasik. Besides, you're too stringy."

"I know," he said, smirking. "But why risk it? I think we should work together. It's more fun that way."

Sianna nodded. A sly look came over her as she fixed an eye on him. "If you're looking for fun, I know what we can work on together." Her tail curled over his. "What say you?"

His clothes suddenly felt too warm and restrictive, and the bedroom too inviting. Kosk wouldn't be likely to return anytime soon, but it was more comfortable anyway. "I think I have a few ideas. Some of them will be better if we wait."

"Oh?" She leaned in, licking his lips. "For what?"

Despite the contract, the Matriarch, strife at home, and all the other roles and responsibilities of his life, he grinned at her like he didn't have a care in the world. For one night, at least, he wouldn't let himself worry. "Because we both have claws, lover, and I'll need some stronger bedding."

ADRENALINE HIGH

Kandrel

Three miles up and counting. Air's thin. Clouds at my feet. Glass beneath my fingers. Look at the world spinning slowly below. Ground cars below tram rails below hover lanes below city copters. A million little lights skim over the distant surface dotted with old skyscrapers. Like glow-flies between blades of grass.

Wind catches my flaps, but I'm holding tight. Effortlessly. Fingers are tipped with bonded gecko-skin prosthetics. Whatever it had cost (and it hadn't been small) was worth it. Prosthetics for my hands, bionics for my limbs, metal for my bones, and silicon for my brain. Three miles up, and with the smog I'd've been dead two ago if I hadn't had filters in my lungs. New Angelas was not a city friendly to wet tissue.

I stop again to let the hydraulics in my legs cool down. They've carried me this far, but I could feel the steam rising from them. Good job, boys. Take a few minutes off and I'll climb the last few hundred feet under my own power. For the millionth time, I check my wrist. On it is a patch of bare faux-skin kept permanently free of fur where a smart tattoo tracks my progress. Pigments beneath my skin show the whole of Magnolia Tower, all thousand and eight stories tall. It glows through my hide with phospho-luminescence reverse engineered from deep sea fishes. Here I am on the nine-hundredth-and-eighty-third story. Any story now I'd find the right point of entry.

Light flares. Automatic compensation in my implanted retinas dims my vision to preserve my night-sight. Twenty feet to my right an express elevator scythes past at fifty miles per hour, audibly decelerating before it hits the top of the tower. Windows are dimmed. Don't know if anyone can see out. Don't care. It's a dark night with no moon. I don't even need my chameleon suit to be unnoticed, but I'm wearing it anyway, because I'm a fucking professional. That's why, while all those runners down at street-level were sprinting at top speed just to scrape together enough for their next fix, I'm up here getting paid in megacredits.

They didn't hire just anyone for corporate espionage. If I were caught, I'd be a liability. No matter how good a mind-wipe protocol I ran, a talented psyk could still lift enough details from my cranium to link me back to my employer. So instead, the plan is to not be caught at all. Sound good? I think so too. I think that's what I'll do. Just never be caught. Good thing that's what I'm best at. It's what I was designed for—first by being born in the flesh, and second by being born again in metal and silicon and carbon fiber.

Not to say my natural talents weren't significant before I decided to undergo the surgery. I was the son of an ascended, so already I had the jump on the poor skin-walkers I saw everywhere around Magnolia Tower Arcology. Dumb, deaf, blind, weak humans, convinced that their superior intellect and their possession of thumbs somehow made them gods of this earth. Well, more the fool, them. They gave us stupid animals brains, and now we're smarter, faster, and stronger, and wonder of wonder, it turns out thumbs can be artificially implanted!

Mom hadn't been a fan of the modifications. What can you expect from a first-gen like her? Her parents had been sugar gliders au-naturale, barely more than zoo specimens. Then Agri-corp happened, and all the animals caught the smarts. Even so, she'd been a naturalist. Only ever wanted things the way they'd been grown, rather than the way they'd been made. Natural food, so scrawny fruits and discolored vegetables from organic farmers when we could buy perfect tomatoes and genetically superior bananas from the local store at a quarter of the price. Natural scents, so our little mid-story hole smelled worse than the factory-reprocessed air outside. Natural friends and natural neighbors, so clothes were a rarity. I'd had my education in the sugar glider anatomy by an early age. Dad hadn't even been ascended, so I guess her sex life had been "natural" too. I guess I should be grateful that she'd gone to see a doctor when she'd been with me and my two sisters, or we might have come out stupid hybrids. Life's not so good for the sub-sentient these days, so I have that to be thankful for at least.

She'd even given me a name she said was native to the region where we were from. Djarrtjuntjun. Hell, I can't even pronounce it, and it's mine. I don't care if it's traditional—it's unusable. Had she given me anything of actual worth?

Well, yes. Everything, really. Don't think I'm ungrateful. She gave me all the tools that made me what I was today. Sleek fur? I call it natural insulation. Webs arm-to-leg? Watch me fly. Tail as long as I am high? It's called a rudder. Freakishly large eyes? All the better to see you with, dear. All my cybernetics just enhanced what I already had, improving them from the home-grown variety of breaking-and-entering tools to an industrial-grade cybersafe-cracker mounted on biological wings. You should see me work. I'm a piece of fucking art.

And they pay. Diamond earrings and gold connectors for my craniojack pay. Premium vat-bred caviar and designer synthetic champagne pay. I live like a king among gliders. I'm the duke of flaps. They call me petauridae superioris. I call myself Jun. And if you're not pulling in a corporate bankroll, no, you can't afford me.

Two stories up the side of the arcology and I see darkened glass. Hand on the window emits ultrasonic vibrations, too high for the security microphones to catch. Vibrations come back. A map forms. Executive office. Perfect. In the window frame are vibration sensors. A short electromagnetic pulse fries them without setting off the alarm. In the corner across the room, a motion tracking infrared camera. Ultraviolet kilowatt laser through the darkened glass burns out its vision.

Prosthetic fingers cut the glass and I'm in, scampering through the sharp hole. I make sure not to catch my sensitive webbing on the glass. Blood would be too identifiable. Nice comfy executive chair behind a desk way too large for any human to actually fill, but that didn't matter. Other than the holomonitor display, it was completely empty. Why did he pay a secretary, if not to have the full desk for him. I hop down. Plush carpet beneath my feet.

There's probably other smaller motion detectors, too small for my scan to catch, but they won't catch me. I'm far too small. Stupid executives still stuck twenty years in the past, when corporate espionage didn't break into your nine-hundredth floor office on four legs and webbed wings in a package no larger than one of their soda cans. Their old security just wasn't built to catch me.

I find the computer jack built into the CEO's desk. In my backpack are multi-jack adapters. It takes me a minute to find one that fits, then another to hook up the interfaces. I don't bother "hacking". It's not necessary. It never was. I count on one truism: business people hate computers. They're finicky. They're logical. And every month, just like clockwork, they tell you that your old password just isn't good enough anymore, and you have to come up with a whole new one! How inconvenient!

The desk has drawers. They're locked, but it has old keyholes rather than electronic locks. The keyholes are so large I can almost fit my hand inside. It's pup's play to align the tumblers and push the drawer open. In the top one, just where I expected them to be, are post-it notes. On each one is a litany of profane worship to the gods of cybersecurity.

"ThisIsAPassword123!"

"WhyDoIHaveToChangeThisAgain5?"

"OkayJamesThisIsANewPassword4."

"StopBuggingMe99"

All arranged in reverse chronological order, they go on for years, one a month, and occasionally more frequently when poor mister personal-jet-and-weekends-in-the-Seychells-CEO forgot his password. Again. And again.

I follow the chain to its miserable end, then log into the system with "ThisIs25CharactersOrMoreSoStopTellingMeToMakeANewOne." I'm in. Why bother with high-end hacking software when you've got a low-end user?

I'm in and out in seconds. It wouldn't matter what account I'd hijacked. Accessing *these* files is about to get me some serious attention. Their security net will be programmed to recognize the CEO's behavior patterns, and he was about to misbehave. Four point two zetabytes in under two seconds into cranial storage. When I disconnect, the first silent alarm is already flashing red beneath the CEO's table.

Back out through the window. At this altitude the air is freezing, but my chameleon suit has enough insulation that, with my fur, I don't even notice it. I have a graceful swan dive, and from three miles up, I figure I can get a good amount of speed towards distant freedom before the aerial patrols catch up.

My heart beats. Man I love this feeling. Air screaming past at fifty miles per hour. If I want to go any faster, I'd have to get out and push. Or get rocket boots.

Now there's an idea. I'll add it to the list.

Clouds approach. Then tear at my cheeks as I dive through water crystals and solidified smog. In a second I'm through, and the distant needle spires of New Angelas rise up to meet me. Before I draw level with even the highest one, the sound of choppers is in the air. Unmanned drones. Those aren't a danger. Their radar can't pick out something as small as me. I'm out. I'm golden.

I'm free.

A blip in my retinal hud. Click. Click. Sonar.

I'm doomed.

I extend all four legs. Thin flaps of skin catch the air and slow my descent in a graceful curve. I angle my forelegs for evasive action, twisting left and right. Click. Click. It's too soft and too quick for my ears to catch, but my neural wetware informs me that it did, indeed, see me.

Shit. Okay, give me info. Satellite connection grants me an uplink, and my query is sent on the next packet. Glance at my wrist, and tumble into a freefall as the gesture ruins my glide. It's okay, I have time to pull back up. Novacorp. The security firm on duty tonight is Novacorp, and now I'm logged into their internal net. Next query is away as I dip below the highest skyscrapers and pull my tail spin into a fast glide in between the towering penthouses. Whoever is on my tail is close. I can hear the sonar now, audible clicks above the rushing wind.

Something whooshes past me, and only wired reflexes lets me tuck my wings and roll. I catch my first glimpse against the under-lit clouds. A sharp collection of curves and points, about ninety percent wings. A bat. Of course they've got a bat on payroll.

I level out and duck around a building as it scythes past. An updraft catches my flaps and pulls me upwards twenty feet back to the apex of a building. I sprint across the abandoned rooftop and throw myself from the far side. I'm fast, but the bat is a better flyer. Wings envelop me. There's another moment of freefall, then breath is knocked from me as we collide into the glass window of someone's penthouse apartment. Of course, the bat's impact is cushioned by my body. Asshole.

"Don't resist. You are under arrest."

With the updraft roaring around us, even his shouting sounds like a whisper in my ears. My wrist buzzes and I glance down. Only one bat on roster at Novacorp. Hire date within the last week. Just my fucking luck. Arthur Jenkins. And it—and *he* has his wings around me. I send my next query off while I struggle against him. He's a flying fox, one of the fuzzy ones with a face that doesn't immediately make me think of early black-and-white movie monsters. His ears wiggle in the wind. It's actually rather warm in his wings. If only he wasn't trying to fit handcuffs to my wrists with one spare foot. Time. I just need time.

His fumbling with the cuffs gives me the opening I needed. He doesn't know I have hard-wired actuators in my legs for high jumps. I catch the look of surprise on his face when the frilly little sugar glider he's caught pushes with the force of industrial hydraulics and launches back into the night.

That's a mistake he won't make twice.

Response hits my wrist at the same time his sonar ripples over me again. I've got his Citizens Identification Pin. I bless the back-door I'd bought into the registration bureau. Next query might take a while, so I fire it off as I'm gliding in between two towers. I'm close enough to ground level now that I can figure my location by the tops of buildings. Fifth and Walnut. I turn right.

Arthur is on me again, one clawed wingtip holding onto my ankle. It throws both of us into freefall, but he uses the time to crawl up and secure me with his legs. With my wing-flaps squeezed to my sides, I've got zero say on where we fly.

His wings snap open, and it feels like I've been punched when momentum drives his feet into my diaphragm. He slams me into a second building as I'm gasping. I feel him fumbling for the cuffs again as I'm attempting to catch my breath. When I start to struggle again, he leans forward and bites my neck. Well, there goes the whole vampire cliche.

"Arthur," I wheeze. With the wind gusting past, he doesn't hear me. My lungs won't expand. I can't breathe. I struggle more, and his teeth sink deeper. Fuck, if he weren't trying to arrest me, I'd make him buy me a drink first. "Arthur! Stop!"

That time he hears it. His eyes shoot open and teeth disengage. He's managed to latch one of my forelegs with his cuffs, but he fumbles and drops it loose when he hears his name. "How the fuck?"

Just enough of a distraction. It takes him a few seconds to recover when I duck out of his stunned grip and glide towards nearby freedom.

Freedom doesn't last long, but it's long enough for me to laser his cuffs off and drop them into the yawning gulf below. We're now down to the level of the older skyscrapers. The wind starts to fade as I curve to the left and dip into the cover of an overhanging bit of brickwork. Gecko-finger prosthetics grip the stone with ease.

Sonar pings, followed by radar and ladar. Damn. Seems my date has a few tricks of his own. With a scrabble of claws, he swings upside down into the gap I'd hidden in. "I don't know who you are or how you know my name, but—"

"Arthur. Arthur Jenkins."

"Shut up. You have the right to remain silent. Anything you say—"

"Give it up. That shit hasn't been legal for decades." I try to edge around him, but he blocks my path. He's bigger than me. Faster than me. I glide, but he flies. Guess I'm down to my brain.

"Arthur, check your HUD, if you would be so kind."

He stalls on his approach. Then goes rigid.

"That..."

"That's twenty-five thousand credits. In your account already."

His mouth closes, then opens again. Correction: I'm down to my brain and my bank account.

"I— I can't—"

"Of course not! What was I thinking?" I thumb my wrist. "That's far too low for an officer of your caliber."

I add a zero. He loses his grip with one claw and flails in the air momentarily. I'm silently thankful that this particular rent-a-cop wasn't familiar with black market rates for top corp data.

I launch off while he was regaining his balance. The old Haymarket building is three blocks away, and there's more than enough places to hide there. Plus, I have a stash hidden on the roof, and a few tools that'll guarantee my safe exit from the scene.

Before I even turn the next corner, I feel a tingle as sonar washes over me again. Fuck. Wings surround me, and I meet my third building wall face-first with Arthur spooning in behind me.

"Did you think I was dim? You've already paid. I've got your money, whether I catch you or not. And here I am thinking a collar would look really good on my record."

"For fuck's sake, Arthur, you watch too many cop movies."

He bites my neck again, forcing a gasp out of me. But while I'm definitely caught, he's also not trying to fit another pair of cuffs, or struggling to restrain my forelegs. Oh, I get it. This isn't my first rodeo. This isn't an arrest—it's a negotiation.

"How silly of me. What was I thinking?"

He gives me enough room to reach for my wrist again. I hesitate. It looks good to hesitate—as if I'm not sure I can afford it. It makes him think that I'm giving him a *lot* of money. Then I add another zero. Two point five million credits. He smiles. His eyes light up. I act nervous.

It's not even a quarter of what I'm getting paid.

"You know I still can't just let you go."

I frown and finger my *other* backup—a miniature tazer. I didn't want to pull it out. From this height, it'd be quite lethal. But I've given him every chance to turn back. Come on, Arthur, be smart.

"We'll have to make it look like you just barely escaped. So, shall we dance?"

Ah, an exhibition match, just for the look of it. Now that I could do. On the shoulder of his minimal uniform I could see his personal camera—lense cracked and body crushed. It must have met an unfortunate accident with his rough takedown. So it was just incidental security cameras dotted around the city he wanted to make a show for. I thumb my hidden holster closed again. Sleep tight, dear tazer. Your skills are not needed tonight. I stick my nose right up under his chin. "What, think you can keep up?"

He makes room for me to escape, and I glide across 8th towards the Lyon's Mutual building. He's closing in on me when I latch myself to the stonework on the corner. His wings surround me, and his teeth are at my neck again.

I'm not sure when the silent agreement was made. Was it something I said? I moan as he licks at the bleeding wound he's left me. His uniform has been unzipped down the front, and I can feel him pushing up behind me.

"What the hell? I didn't say—"

"You don't have to." He pushes his nose through my fur. "You've been reeking of it since I first plowed you into a window."

"It's just an adrenaline rush!" I crawl out from beneath him, scaling up the sheer rock.

And that puts his snout just beneath my tail as he follows. Oh, fuck, that feels good. How much tongue does this guy have? A hook-like claw catches my foot as he steadies himself.

I don't know how long he's down there, but I sorely feel his absence when he stops. I glance back at him. He's smiling up at me. "Oh, so I guess that's a no, then?"

Fucker. I put a foot on his face and kick off. Of course it's not a no, dipshit. Not if you've got a tongue like that. But you gotta earn it! Without saying any of this, I angle myself across the road again. He strafes me, as if just to prove he could have me at any time. Oh, and to show off, I'm sure. He's sticking out of his sheath.

I've never had a bat before. I didn't know what to expect, but now that I'm looking at it, it's raising more questions than it's going to solve. For example, where is he expecting me to *fit* all of that? When I land again and he covers me in the blanket of his wings, I lean back. His claws catch on the brickwork. I'm not worried. He can clearly support my weight. He grooms my ears as I pull him up between my legs so I can get a close look at it. Fucking hell. It takes both of my hands to fit around it, and it sticks up straight to the top of my belly. Not bad at all.

Arthur holds on tight to the building as I stroke. When he throbs I can feel that length tensing against my thighs and firming against my stomach. It twitches out of my fingers and sprays up along my chameleon suit. He's breathing heavily against the top of my head. A second splash hits the underside of my chin and drips down over my chest. Oh man, this bat is the gift that keeps on giving. I put my hands over his tip, and he shoots straight through my fingers. It spatters my face and drips from the bricks. I open my mouth to lick at my quickly dampening face. He doesn't taste too bad. A bit sweet beneath the bitter, and no aftertaste.

"Shit. Sorry, I—" He manages to gasp in between breaths.

"Hair trigger when you're flying?" I ask. He nods. "It's the adrenaline. I get it too."

"Don't worry, it won't take me long to go again."

"Hah!" I laugh in his face. "That's if you can catch me again!"

I duck under his wing. He's not trying to keep me still anymore, and this time I angle myself for the Haymarket.

The wind pulls drips and streamers of bat spunk from my fur as I glide. Where does he keep it all?

He tackles me to the side and flaps twenty meters over the first layer of hovercar traffic to a half-finished high-rise. It's been just a skeletal steel structure for years, ever since the towering corporate arcologies started to dominate the sky. This time he rolls me onto a horizontal surface made of scaffolding boards. Three of his limbs stilt around me while his right wing drags his strange wing-digit down my front. I spread my legs for him, and his curled claw catches the zipper just beneath my tail. He tugs, spilling fur and rump and balls and my own poking length out into the night air.

"Aww, it's so cute!" He laughs.

"Fuck off, cop. You're not—" I stop mid-sentence as his long tongue curls three times around my shaft. "—fuck."

He laughs through his mouthful. Okay. Maybe not a whole mouthful. Guess I'm just not built to measure up to a bat—in more ways than one. I drag my hands over his ears. He hums under his breath. That *vibrates*. I never stood a chance. His tongue slides against my cock and dips down beneath my balls. That thing has applications I could never have anticipated. I convulse as I spray the roof of his mouth. He's kind. He doesn't let go until he's drained me of every drop.

He's hard again. Twitching between my spread legs and dribbling more of that fluid onto my belly. He throbs visibly, lifting from my stomach and slapping against his own front. Then it drops again, making a "splat" sound as it lands in my wet fur.

I turn and scamper. Three steps and I'm over empty space again. I duck beneath the first hover-lane, weaving through traffic at speed. His sonar caresses me. A truck screams past between us. I catch a slow-going taxi and use the momentum to flip over the next lane. I laugh. This is how it should be. This is *life!* Behind me, Arthur dodges a bus and disappears momentarily behind a slowing tow truck. When I see him again, he's beneath the sports car strapped to the back of the flatbed. He launches himself at me. I can see his crazed smile even through the night time gloom, punctuated by the blinding glares of low altitude traffic.

I dodge, he weaves. I'm not at my most aerodynamic, because I'm hard again. It's the rush. It's the height. It's the adrenaline pumping through my veins as his claw catches my ankle again and sends me into an uncontrolled spin. I get my flaps out in the wind just in time to dodge a car. Asshole. Sonar brushes my fur again. I can't even see him, but I can sense his presence. I'm stiffer than I ever remember being.

He nails me against the side of an apartment complex. The lights are on. Someone's watching TV. I don't care. Arthur's behind me, and he's wet and slick. He grinds my crotch against the window as he pushes his twitching tip up under my tail. I leave a smear on the glass when he spreads me around his slim tip. That doesn't feel so bad.

It's followed by what feels like whole inches of cock. Oh fuck, I can't take this. He bites my neck when I cry out. Someone's watching us through the glass. I hope they get a good show. Hell, where am I supposed to fit all of this bat? He keeps pushing, and he keeps biting. Even though I've just cum, I can't help it. I start to wash down the confused onlooker's window. It dribbles down the glass translucent and flowing in thin waves as Arthur slams my prostate.

It's too much. I need a break. I push, and reluctantly Arthur let me go. I feel him slide out of me. And keep sliding out. I close my eyes. It's too much, but it also feels good. Really good. Even though I'm pushing away, I'm really sort of regretting it as I feel his tip finally slip out.

And then he's twitching against my back, and then I'm pushing off of the unlucky audience member's window. Between the top layer of hover traffic and the raised rails of the tram network, I glide to the wall of the Haymarket. I've lost too much altitude to catch the roof, but it wouldn't take too much time to climb up to it.

Arthur lands around me. This time, he's gentle. He licks the multiple punctures he's given me as he slides between my rump cheeks. I twitch my tail against him and one free wing hugs me like a tight, constricting blanket. I let go of the wall entirely and let gravity slowly slide me down onto him. He doesn't move this time—letting me grow used to as much of the length as I can accommodate. I look down. There must be half of that throbbing giant twitching in the air between my legs rather than inside me. Then I feel him push against a curve of my inner walls, and both of us know that's as far as he goes.

His wing hugs me tight, and his hips pull back. I lean myself into his hug. I close my eyes and let my head loll. It feels like I'm flying again as he thrusts. There's so much of him, it feels like he's humping through all of me, rather than just the little bit my rational brain knows I've been able to fit. It doesn't matter. The sensation is electric.

He's breathing raggedly into my ears. I reach up and wrap my fingers around his head. He leans down and puts his tongue to work. It's long enough that he can stroke me with it, even while his larger body curls around mine and slides that monster of his through my sensitive ring.

Then he's throbbing. The tug is so strong that it moves my body, pulling me back against his belly with each pulse of his shaft inside me. A hot rush fills me to and beyond full. I can feel it gushing out against my thighs and dripping over his sheath. If there wasn't room for the first soaking spray, then there definitely isn't room for the second. Or the third.

His tongue squeezes. I think I'm cumming, but I can't tell. Maybe it's a dry orgasm. There's so much of his cum in my fur I can't tell. Three times in probably just as many minutes, that's definitely a record for me. His wing holds me as he humps straight through his own peak. The gushes of liquid still running between where I'm trying to clench around him suggest that he's enjoying the treatment thoroughly.

Then he's softening. I can feel it in the way the throbbing fades and his thrusting pulls more out than it pushes back in. And then he throbs free. His last couple of twitches splash my back, warm through my chameleon suit. Man, I'm going to need to dry-clean this. Or I can just buy another. I could buy another ten with tonight's pay.

He doesn't stop me as I crawl up to the roof. I sit on the concrete rim, looking out into the city. He joins me a moment later. Bats aren't particularly agile on flat surfaces. He climbs wing over wing to me, then stops at my side and leans heavily into me. I have to brace to not be knocked over.

"So. How often do you steal shit? I think I'm free tomorrow night."

I laugh. Oh man, I really caught a gem. Or is it the other way around?

"Um, seriously. I'm not sure how I'm going to explain this, though. By all rights I really should have caught you.

I nod and run my hand over his head. His big ears twitch against my fingers.

"Arthur, do you trust me?" I ask.

"No." He didn't have to give it much thought.

"That's fair." And then I taze him.

His whole body goes rigid, and when my juice runs out, he collapses on the edge of the roof. He's breathing. Good. I reach down and kiss his head. I waddle over to the stash I have under a broken roof tile near the north side. First, I extract a little kit I keep just for situations like this. Well, sort of like this. Usually it's tranqs, or a graze from a bullet. An injection of pain killers. Fuck, I'm already starting to feel sore. I swear I can still feel him inside me. I think I'm still dripping. I look down into a puddle. No, I'm *definitely* still dripping. I start to zip back up, then stop. Actually, it's probably better if I let it air a bit, rather than have it get trapped inside the suit. Less to clean.

Second, I have a little wide-band white noise generator that I *would* have brought with me if I'd known I was going to face a real predator of a cop like Arthur. Not that I'm regretting it. Not even a second of it. I walk back over to him, attaching the device to my suit. When I fly away, I might as well be invisible in a sea of noise. Not that I think I'll need it now, but it's always good to be sure. Anyway, it gives him a better story.

I reach down and caress his balls from behind. They still felt heavy. I wish I had more of the night. Ah well. Maybe there'll be a next time. "Sorry Arthur, but this really is for your benefit. Tell them you chased me this far before you got tazed. A perfect alibi. Not only do you get to keep my two and a half mil, but you might even make it off without even a disciplinary. Hell, play it right and maybe you'll even get a raise."

I turn to the roof's edge, but before I leap, I have another idea. I wire him a bit more money. Only five digits this time. 13092 creds. Hardly a drop in the pool compared to his night's haul. But maybe worth more in the long run. Because if he types that into the right New Angelas exchange, he'll get my personal com on my wrist. It's a risk, but it's a risk I'm willing to take.

Then I launch myself into the night. Four point two zetabytes of paydata in my cranium and one amazing fling still dripping from me as I glide off below traffic. A note to my fixer says I'm ready to exchange.

Smart money would buy me a transfer to another city. This payout is enough to survive on for years. But I don't want to survive. I want to live, and there wasn't anything quite as alive as the skyline of the New Angelas sprawl, broken up by the arcologies towering high into the sky. Maybe if I hit the right clients, I'll get another visit from Novacorp securities, and the only cop they've got on payroll that could ever catch me.

Hell, I'm rich now. I'm genuinely fucking minted. Maybe next time, he'll let me catch him instead.

About the Authors

Of The Wilds

Of The Wilds is a fantasy author who lives in the United States. He's come a long way from a dragon-obsessed childhood, to a dragon-obsessed adulthood. Tired of seeing dragons used as monsters and plot devices, he decided to use them as main characters, instead. Beyond writing, his passions include progressive music, good food, and great beer.

Of The Wilds has been writing since his Dragonlance fanfic days in middle school, but hopes he's gotten a little better along the way. Nowadays he enjoys short stories, but his focus is on fantasy novels. Though he's been writing them for over a decade, only recently has he shared his work with the world. His characters frequently include both dragons and humans, along with gryphons, and a variety of creatures unique to his fantasy universe.

He's often found wasting time on Twitter as @OfTheWilds, where he pretends to be a dragon dreaming he's a coyote. You can find a collection of his stories and novels in progress at his SoFurry page, http://of-the-wilds.sofurry.com.

He would like to dedicate this story to his parents. While he may never let them read it, they have always supported his every endeavor, and for that, he will be eternally grateful. And to his readers, wherever they may be, thank you.

Whyte Yoté

Whyte Yoté has been writing for the furry fandom since 2000, and has worked with Sofawolf, FurPlanet, Bad Dog Books, and Rabbit Valley to publish the 31 feathers in his cap. His work can be found in Heat Magazine, the FANG and ROAR series, and numerous other series and one-off books of short stories.

He currently lives in Sacramento, California with his forever boyfriend of 13 years, Tym.

For a complete bibliography, go to http://www.furaffinity.net/journal/2827074/

Resolute

Resolute is an author from the US Midwest. While he isn't a gryphon yet, there's always hope. His love of fantastic creatures and great art brought him to the furry fandom. When not writing or reading, he enjoys music, bad puns, games, baking, terrible puns, and the occasional convention.

Resolute's voracious appetite for reading and (over)active imagination led him to the writing desk. In spite of its reputation, fanfic helped develop and encourage his craft until he created his own original work featuring a human and gryphon partnership-turned-romance. "Nothing Feathered, Nothing Gained" takes place concurrently with that story series, starting with Feathers with Benefits; while the characters may never meet, both couples steer by the world's winds of change. Resolute also writes standalone short stories and novellas, with a novel or three in early planning.

You can find him on Twitter @ResoluteRL, or on SoFurry at https://resolute.sofurry.com/

Kandrel

Kandrel is an American red fox who's adopted the United Kingdom as his new home. He's been a proud member of the fandom for well over two decades, and is, now that he thinks about it, starting to become rather self-conscious about his age. Why did you do this to him? Now he's plucking at his grey whiskers. In your insistence to know more about him, you've started him down this nightmarish spiral of self-doubt and destruction. I hope you're happy with yourself.

Kandrel's writing has been entertaining fans in a variety of inappropriate ways for years now. He's a particularly avid proponent of the one true genre, science fiction (naturally). In five years, he hopes to be a wealthy, adored, and cherished author who is given praise and worship wherever his feet tread. In lieu of that lofty goal, he'd actually be happy with a few belly rubs once in a while and a "Good Boy" when he manages to get a story in on time for submission.

You can find most of his work linked from his own website at http://www.foxyonline.com or at his sofurry account at http://kandrel.sofurry.com. You can find his lewd and lascivious game Savannah at http://humpin.gs.